Sam and I would live forever. . . .

We rode far and fast. We cut through the thick, wet afternoon air till bumps rose on my arms and I shivered against Sam's back. I closed my eyes and let my mind fill with the noise of the engine and mental pictures of Sam's bike flying through the air that hot afternoon in the grove.

I could die right here, I thought.

We sliced around a wide curve, and the earth tugged at us. It was like a roller coaster, but without the smug certainty you'd be all right. I tried to hang on to the electric buzz in my throat. That was what thinking you might die felt like. That was what Izzy was feeling.

I tried to hang on to the feeling, but it left me. All I felt was the rush of freedom, the empty place where worry should have been. We rolled down that road and I felt like we would live forever, Sam and I, and I hated myself for feeling it.

Don't miss any of the books in *Love Stories*
—a romantic new series from Bantam Books!

Love Stories

Sharing Sam

KATHERINE APPLEGATE

BANTAM BOOKS
NEW YORK · TORONTO · LONDON · SYDNEY · AUCKLAND

RL 6, age 12 and up

SHARING SAM

A Bantam Book / February 1995

Produced by Daniel Weiss Associates, Inc.
33 West 17th Street
New York, NY 10011

ISBN: 0-553-56660-1

Published simultaneously in the United States and Canada

Bantam Books are published by Bantam Books, a division of Bantam
Doubleday Dell Publishing Group, Inc. Its trademark, consisting of the
words "Bantam Books" and the portrayal of a rooster, is Registered in
U.S. Patent and Trademark Office and in other countries. Marca
Registrada. Bantam Books, 1540 Broadway, New York, New York 10036.

PRINTED IN THE UNITED STATES OF AMERICA

OPM   0 9 8 7

For Ann Brashares.
Thanks. Again.

And, as always,
for Michael.

Chapter One

SOME PEOPLE SAID Sam had robbed a Get n' Go in Okeechobee. Some said he was an undercover narc. A reliable source in the girls' bathroom claimed he was Mick Jagger's illegitimate son. We were bored with our gentle lives, and dark, silent Sam was the object of much speculation. As the new guy at school and the only male in AP Bio to sport a black leather jacket, he was asking for it.

Sam rode a motorcycle, no helmet. In the sea of entry-level Chevy sedans and sober parentmobiles, the big Harley in Student Lot B commanded attention. It spoke of mangled limbs, decapitations, promising lives cut short. Conjugating verbs from my window seat in Spanish class, I couldn't take my eyes off it.

I suppose, given that Harley, not to mention the

1

rumors, that it didn't surprise me when I happened, one Monday after school, to witness Sam Cody's inevitable demise.

I was sitting under a tree in the middle of an orange grove near my house. Snickers, my Arabian mare, was grazing nearby. The day, warm and clear, dazzled like a prism. I had my history textbook open on my lap, which I figured was almost the same thing as reading it.

I went to the grove from time to time—sometimes to study, more often to daydream. The star of my reveries was Lance Potts, the golden-boy-blue-eyed-honor-society-junior-class-president-football-center guy I'd fantasized about for months, practicing pillow kisses after *SNL* on Saturday nights. Although Lance had no idea I existed, he was always kind enough to make an appearance in my daydreams at a moment's notice.

But lately, Sam Cody had been making unscheduled appearances in them as well. I was not sure what to make of this development. Sam was not, after all, the kind of guy I was attracted to.

Although, to be fair, Sam did have very nice eyes.

The hoarse whine of a motorcycle broke the stillness. I tossed my book aside. This was not a bike trail. Technically, it wasn't even a horse trail. Yelling a few expletives, I dashed out to the narrow dirt road that bisected the grove. Then I saw the black jacket, the too-long hair, and I knew it was Sam.

It was one thing to ponder Sam's dark history

over a bowl of Orville Redenbacher Light on a dateless Friday evening. It was quite another thing to be trapped in the middle of nowhere with him, armed only with my pepper spray, the one my mom had stuck in the toe of my stocking the Christmas before.

"Hey!" I screamed. "Get off the trail!"

Suddenly, as if he'd reined it in at my command, the bike bucked and twisted. It careened off the trail, carving a clean arc in the still air. Sam clung to it like a bronco rider as the bike plummeted to the ground near an orange tree. It somersaulted once before coming to a stop.

The Harley silenced, the field came alive again with chirps, buzzes, whirs. I waited, hoping for a moan, some sign he'd survived.

Nothing.

As I ran to the wreck I steeled myself for the bloodied corpse and lifeless stare, the horror-movie scenes from those driver ed movies. I conjured up pages from my first-aid book. A, B, C: A was airway, B was breathing, but what the heck was C?

The grass stirred.

Sam was wrapped around the twisted carcass of his bike. A tiny trickle of blood made its way down his left temple.

He opened his eyes. "This isn't hell, is it?"

I shook my head, incredibly relieved that he was alive.

"Florida," I said.

"Close enough."

"I'm here to rescue you," I said nervously. "Don't move."

I leaned close to check his eyes. If his pupils were dilated, that was a bad thing, although I couldn't remember why. Close up, his face was all angles and planes, a geometry lesson. His eyes were nearly black, thick brows, thick lashes. I couldn't be sure about the pupil situation. I caught the faint, acrid smell of tobacco. It figured he would smoke.

I examined a gash on his left hand. "You have a death wish or something?" I muttered.

He touched his bloody temple and swore. "I blew a damn tire. I can't believe it. I just changed that tire two weeks ago! Oh, man, this sucks."

"I mean, why don't you wear a helmet, for God's sake? It's the law. Plus," I added, "you smoke."

Sam stared at me as if I weren't quite in focus. "I'm lying here bleeding to death, and you're *nagging* me?"

"I hope you realize how lucky it is you landed in a hunk of grass. It could have been a hunk of rock."

"Lucky. Yeah."

"Don't move, I have to think. I took first aid in Girl Scouts, but that was seven years ago."

Sam started to pull his leg free. He winced.

"Stop!" I cried. "Don't move the victim."

"*I'm* not the victim," he said, stroking a twisted fender.

I checked his head wound. It was bleeding, all right, although not very dramatically. I needed something to bind the cut. There was only one thing to do. I took off my T-shirt. Fortunately, I had a bathing suit top on underneath.

"Maybe I'm in heaven after all," Sam said.

I tried to rip the T-shirt with my teeth. It always works in the movies.

The movies, it just so happens, are full of crap.

"I'm Sam Cody, by the way."

"I know," I said, and was instantly sorry. Strictly speaking, there was no reason I should know his name.

"And you're Alison Chapman."

I blinked, my mouth full of T-shirt. Strictly speaking, there was no reason he should know my name.

I could feel my throat starting to blotch. It was tacky to flirt while binding a wound.

"I'm just going to tie this sucker around your head," I said. Before he could fuss I crouched behind him, folded the shirt into a long strip, and tied it around his forehead. The back of his hair curled sweetly over his collar.

"Ow." He winced. "Just my luck I get the Brownie paramedic."

I stood, brushed off my knees, and admired my handiwork. "You may go into shock at any moment," I said. "I think I'm supposed to cover you with a blanket."

"You could use your jeans," he suggested helpfully.

"I'm going to go get my horse. I'll put her

blanket over you, then ride for help. But you have to promise not to move—"

"Time out." Before I could stop him, Sam pulled free of his bike and struggled to his feet. "This is getting way too weird."

"I told you not to stand. You've had a brush with death."

"You did say horse?"

"Snickers. She's over there, under a tree. This is a horse trail, no bikes allowed."

"I was just passing through," he said. "It's a great shortcut to the highway."

"Didn't you see the sign?"

"Yeah, it said No Trespassing. What's your excuse?"

"I trespassed on a horse, at least."

"Can your horse do one twenty?"

"No." I kicked his blown-out tire. "But neither can your bike anymore."

Suddenly he looked infinitely sad, and I felt like a jerk.

"Look, if you're not going to sit here and wait for an ambulance, let me at least give you a ride," I said.

"I don't do horses. Look, thank you for saving my life. If you need someone to testify for your merit badge, give me a call. But I'm cool." He yanked off the T-shirt. It was smeared with blood. "Sorry," he said. "I'll buy you another one. I'm a little short on cash right now, though."

He stared at the bike forlornly. I wondered if I'd

ever looked at anything with that much longing.

"I'm sure it can be fixed," I said.

"Maybe."

"You know someone who can tow it?"

"I'll figure something out." He took off his black jacket and slung it over his shoulder. I noticed a little plastic packet of Kleenex in one of the pockets. It seemed so incongruous that I grinned. Somehow I'd expected something more sinister.

"What?"

"Nothing. I mean, just . . . your Kleenex."

He blinked. "My what?"

"Nothing."

"Well . . . Nice bleeding on you."

He limped off down the trail. His scuffed boots made little dust clouds. Sam Cody, of the wild speculation and hushed rumors, who had maybe killed a man or robbed a bank or sold substances door to door, and I don't mean vacuums.

Still, he looked sort of pathetic, his metal steed dead by the wayside.

By the time I caught up with him he was nearly to the tree where Snickers was tied. "Come on," I said. "You might as well hitch. We're going the same way."

Sam stopped. His hair was matted where the blood had dried. He looked very tired. "Look, I don't even know you."

"You know my name."

"Sixth-period study hall. Two rows up, one seat

over. I'm familiar with the back of your head. Yesterday you wore one of those wormy ponytail things."

"A scrunchie," I confirmed.

He narrowed his eyes. "So how is it that you know my name?"

"I've heard . . . talk."

"What kind of talk?"

"You know. You're the new guy, it's a small school, people talk."

"Yeah. Well." It was obvious he didn't give a damn.

I hesitated. Up close, with the blood, the dirt, the sweat trickling down his temples, he did look more menacing. Older than all the other guys at school, with their dust-bunny mustaches and self-conscious swaggers.

"Have you ever been to Okeechobee?" I asked.

Sam closed his eyes. I had the feeling I was wearing him out. He swayed slightly, and the Girl Scout in me took over.

I grabbed his arm, and he more or less followed along. His skin was damp and hot, but then, it was hot for January. Besides, my hands were sweating, so it's hard to know who was responsible.

Snickers looked him over doubtfully. Sam leaned against the trunk of the tree. His face was gray.

"This is Snickers," I said. "She's old and she's been known to bite. She doesn't like men."

"That's okay. I don't like horses," he said, but he

8

stroked her shoulder anyway. She snorted derisively.

"Here's the deal," I said. I turned the left stirrup for him. "Left foot in here, right leg over, I'll drive. Got it?"

"I have ridden before. My grandfather has a horse. I just like my transportation without teeth."

Sam eased up into the saddle. I stuffed my book in my backpack, handed it to Sam, and climbed up behind him.

"Are you sure you're not going into shock or something?" I asked, taking the reins. "You look sort of . . . well, like you're dying, to be blunt."

"Nothing an aspirin won't cure."

I took it at a walk, afraid to jostle him any more than necessary. Holding the reins necessitated the occasional wrist-to-waist contact. My wrist, his hard, warm waist. I could smell sweat and tobacco and grass and skin, all mixed in with horse. Sounds awful, I know. It wasn't.

We fell into a smooth, gentle back-and-forth roll that was all Snickers's doing. My breasts grazed Sam's back, my thighs his thighs. Sounds harmless, I know. It wasn't.

Something was happening, something I didn't want to think about too hard. I couldn't say why, but I had the feeling Lance Potts was being retired from active daydream duty.

Lance had the résumé, he had the dimpled smile and the blue eyes. But it was Sam who was giving me goosebumps in eighty-degree Florida sunshine.

9

We rode so silently that I half wondered if Sam had lapsed into a coma. When we got to the highway, I reined Snickers to a halt. "I live a mile down," I said. "I could give you a lift to the doctor."

"No doctor," Sam said.

"Why not?"

"No money."

"I could lend—"

Sam hefted himself off the saddle, swinging a leg over Snickers's neck. He landed with a grimace.

"Where do you live, anyway? I wouldn't mind—"

"I'll hitch, thanks."

"You can't hitch."

He looked up, squinting against the afternoon glare. "Oh? Why's that?"

"You'll end up by the side of the road in a mangled heap. Not unlike your motorcycle."

"I'm a big boy. I'll take my chances."

"You take too many chances," I said, doing an uncanny impersonation of my mother. I dismounted and grabbed my pack from Sam. "Here," I said. "Let me at least give you cab money."

"No."

"A quarter for the phone?"

For the first time, Sam smiled. He touched my shoulder. "I'll be okay, Alison."

I momentarily forgot how to respond, so I kept busy digging through my backpack for some cash. While I did, Sam sauntered over to Snickers. He whispered something in her ear, something she must have liked, because normally she won't let a guy within three feet of her head. He leaned close and kissed her gently on the muzzle, and I felt myself coming to some kind of very important decision.

He caught me looking, and I pulled out a ten-dollar bill. "Here," I said. "At least take this."

But by then Sam was already heading down the road, thumb outstretched, sizing up the possibilities whizzing past.

I watched as he grew smaller and smaller, until at last a battered red pickup stopped and Sam hopped into the cab. It roared off, kicking up dust.

I wondered if he would survive the drive, the day, the year. I hoped so, because I had the insane feeling I was in distinct danger of falling in love.

Chapter Two

AS I UNTACKED Snickers in the little barn behind our house, I got rational about the encounter with Sam. I want to be a biologist, and biologists are big on logic. Scientific method and all that. What data did I have about Sam, when you got down to it? That he was from somewhere else. That he showed evidence of a death wish, or at least bad judgment. The Harley, the hitching, the smoking. Not good, but still, it wasn't like he was wrestling alligators at Gator World.

He was in some advanced classes, like Izzy and me, which meant he probably had some smarts, not that I'd seen too much evidence of it. And I'd heard he was cutting classes already. More not good.

On the up side, he wasn't bad-looking.

Okay, so maybe that was an understatement.

Maybe he was startlingly, breathtakingly, mind-bogglingly good-looking. Plus, he carried pocket Kleenex and had kissed my horse.

I buried my face in the smooth warmth of Snickers's mane. Not much to go on. Kleenex and a kiss, and not even my kiss. Not even an intraspecies kiss.

Still, something had happened out there on the highway. The kind of something that felt remarkably like the early stages of the flu. Churning insides, liquid knees, that sort of thing.

It could be the flu, I conceded. Or it could be that I was actually, finally, me of all people, falling in love.

I was certain what falling in love would be like. Love arrived with bells and whistles and flashing lights, sort of like when the fire alarm at school goes off during a math quiz. I mean, you *know* it's happened. And you *want* it to happen, bad. And I'd always known that when I fell in love, it would be just that—a fall, a drop off the World Trade Center, a bungee-cord swan dive off the Skyline Bridge to Tampa.

I'd never actually bungeed, mind you (hey, I'm not insane), but the way my stomach was pinballing around, I was pretty sure this was how it would feel.

But I was having some tiny second thoughts. I'd always assumed that when I did fall in love, it would (a) be with Lance Potts, or some reasonable

13

facsimile thereof, and (b) not be with a guy who smoked, crashed bikes, and may or may not have been the illegitimate son of Mick Jagger.

I was, as the school counselors like to say, conflicted.

I needed somebody to unconflict me.

I needed Izzy.

Science was what had brought Izzy and me together. We'd met at a summer program at Mote Marine, a research lab in Sarasota. I was nine, she was eight, and we were the only participants, male or female, willing to handle a mud snake. *Voilà.* Instant best friends.

Izzy (full name Isabella Cates-Lopez) was brilliant, a real, live, certifiable genius. A Westinghouse semifinalist who'd skipped her freshman year, a genetics whiz, the kind of person whose brain was so far into theoretical stuff that trying to explain it to me was like discussing it with her cat. I was into ecology, species saving, hands-on science. She was theoretical, abstract, head-in-the-ozone.

But it wasn't like we were geeks, exactly. We were normal, nice-looking, red-blooded American high-school juniors who just happened to have been overlooked in the great pairing lottery. Each of us knew her prince would come. We just figured they were taking the scenic route.

At that moment my ten-year-old sister appeared in the doorway. She expertly spun a basketball on her index finger. "You have the most disgusting grin on your face. Sort of like a stoned cow."

"Did Izzy call?" I asked. There was no point in responding to her. Sara was going through an obnoxious phase. Near as I could pinpoint, it had started sometime around conception.

"What am I, your social secretary?" Sara stroked Snickers's chin. "I was shooting hoops."

"She's probably still at the eye doctor," I said. I passed her Snickers's saddle. Sara scowled, but she dropped her basketball and took the saddle into the large storage room that doubled as a tack room.

"Izzy getting glasses?" Sara called.

"Not at this rate," I said. "She has these headaches, and she's gone to, like, three eye doctors, but Iz refuses to believe them when they say she needs glasses."

Sara returned and straddled a bench. "Can I take Snickers out for a while?"

"I just cooled her down, Sara." I led Snickers into her stall. "And you know the deal. You help with feeding and grooming her and mucking out her stall, you can ride her all you want. You don't, no deal."

She sat there practicing her laser-guided hate looks, a shorter, ganglier version of me. Same light brown hair, same gray eyes, same sweet, wholesome looks that made grandmothers pinch my cheek and guys yawn. I didn't hate her the way she seemed to hate me, but then I wasn't ten, the age when you aren't afraid to say what you're really feeling. Around Sara I just felt . . . well, confused. Usually, I had a pretty good instinct for what was going on in other people's heads. But communicating with my little sister was like trying to get through to an annoying, untrainable, occasionally vicious pet.

"Have I mentioned lately that I detest you, Al?" Sara said by way of good-bye.

I went to the tack room and settled on a trunk, breathing in the rich, sweet smell of leather and saddle soap. I pushed four, Izzy's speed-dial number on the portable phone. Lauren, Izzy's mom, answered. Izzy was at the library, she told me. Her voice was subdued, soft around the edges. I could hear sobbing in the background, punctuated by Spanish.

"Is that Rosa?" I asked, a flutter of worry in my stomach. Rosa was Izzy's Cuban aunt, who shared their waterfront condo.

"Yes, dear."

Lauren never called me "dear." It wasn't her style. "Is everything all right?"

"I have to go now. Isabella's at the library. You can talk to her there." A fresh wail in the background. "Really, now, I have to go."

I listened to the dial tone. Someone must have died, was all I could figure. One of Rosa's relatives back in Cuba, maybe. Izzy's dad, a well-known fiction writer, had come to the United States from Cuba many years ago. Her mother, who'd edited his books for the U.S. market, had helped arrange the whole thing. It was all very romantic, I thought. First to fall in love with his ideas, his words. Then him. Very bigger-than-life.

I grabbed the keys to the station wagon and promised my mom I'd be back in time for dinner.

Way back when, my parents, who shared a thriving veterinary practice, had used the aging wagon for occasional emergencies. It had once even played ambulance for a goat who'd eaten a Tupperware tub full of lentil pilaf. It smelled a little rank, but I'd convinced my parents to keep it around as an extra family car. It wasn't the sexiest transportation on earth, but at least I had wheels.

The New College library was virtually empty; it was almost dinnertime. I found Izzy at her usual carrel, a nice corner spot without the distraction of a window view. She was hunched over, her long hair obscuring her face. I envied Izzy's beauty sometimes, the exotic darkness from her father, the fragile intensity from her mother. Her face was long, her eyes deep-set. She was tall, very tall, and elegant without being self-conscious. It was an intimidating beauty, one that seemed to keep guys at bay. Still, I would have given anything to slip into her skin for a day.

Piles of books, thick ones with wordy titles,

filled the carrel. I dropped my backpack on one of them. "Iz," I said, "what's the most bizarre thing on earth I could tell you?"

She looked up from a book. Her eyes were bloodshot. Drops at the ophthalmologist's, probably, but there was something else there that made me uneasy. "You've discovered a cure for cancer," she said.

"You okay, Iz? Is something going on, I mean? I called your house and I could have sworn I heard Rosa crying."

"She's always crying. She cries over that cotton commercial with all the old people."

"That's what I figured." I nodded at the books. "What's the deal? You're not doing some extra-credit stuff for Leach's class, are you? You're going to make the rest of us look like slugs."

"Just a little light reading." Her voice was not quite hers, I realized. It was like a message on an answering machine. I scanned the titles. *Principles and Practice of Clinical Oncology. The Merck Manual of Diagnosis and Therapy. Radiation and Chemotherapy: Therapeutic Advances.*

Something began to coil inside me, tightening, twisting, hurting. "Iz?" I said. "What did the eye doctor say?"

Izzy closed her book. "What's the most bizarre thing on earth I could possibly tell you?" she said, and then she began to cry.

*   *   *

I drove Izzy to Turtle Beach, because the sun was going down and the ocean was quiet and it was the only thing I could think of to do.

We went to our usual spot, a gentle dune where we'd watched a loggerhead turtle lay her eggs in the glittering moonlight the previous May.

This was the place where we'd cried over bad grades and parental injustice and unrequited love. We'd discussed the eternal, slippery mystery of the ages—Guys: Why Are They Such Weenies? We'd mapped out college. We'd planned our brilliant careers. We'd written our joint Nobel acceptance speech and named our children (Izzy liked Guinevere, but I figured it was just a phase).

We'd allowed for the occasional setback—the males who resisted women in science, the costs of our education, the juggling of multiple loves on multiple continents.

We'd just never thought to allow for brain cancer.

The sun boiled into the horizon. We buried our feet in the floury sand. Mostly we cried. We did not speak. There were too many questions, no answers.

Izzy finally broke the silence, laughing at two gulls fighting over a piece of seaweed.

At the sound of her deep laugh, I realized I was furious. "Why didn't you tell me?" I demanded in a choked voice. "You *knew,* Iz. You've been going for tests—you weren't going to an eye doctor. That time you got dizzy after PE and said it was your

19

period. . . . You must have thought I was so stupid." I was babbling as tears rolled down my cheeks. "I *was* so stupid. You're my best friend, you jerk."

She turned her placid gaze on me. "Was there a complete thought in there somewhere?"

I felt terrible. Everything I said mattered. This would be the scene where *I Found Out,* and I'd blown it already, yelling at Izzy when she needed me. There could be other scenes, scenes at the hospital, chemo or radiation maybe, and I would have to handle them better. I wanted to do this right, to be there for her until she was okay again.

"God, I'm sorry," I whispered. "I'm a jerk. I just started thinking about you worrying, with no one to talk to, and at least I could have worried with you."

"What point would there have been in both of us freaking?" Izzy asked calmly. "The first two doctors were telling me all kinds of things: it was nerves, it was stress, I needed glasses, I had the flu. And then they did the EEG and the MRI and a bunch of other tests with multiple letters, and the odds were so long that I figured . . ." She shrugged. "There's still plenty of time to worry."

She watched the waves weaving in and out of each other. Then she looked at me, straight on. "Five or six months, anyway."

Five or six. Till summer, then. "You mean, six months until you're all better," I said, hoping I was right, knowing I wasn't.

She shook her head, almost imperceptibly.

20

"Until you're in remission, then."

"Until I'm worm food," Izzy said. She chewed on a thumbnail. "Although one textbook I read said three months, four at the outside. Statistically speaking, that seems to be the norm. It varies a lot, of course. I'm just assuming the worst."

"Shut up, Izzy. Shut up. This is not about statistics. This is you. You are not going to die, not tomorrow, not in four months or six months or six years." I took her hand and held it so hard she winced. "Doctors can be wrong, they're wrong all the time. They tell people this crap and then their patients end up outliving them."

Izzy sighed. "Al, that happened on *The Young and the Restless* last summer."

"Still, you can't know this for sure," I said. "They have to do biopsies. You don't even know if it's malignant yet."

"True. But judging from what I know so far . . . I'm just saying it's likely that the prognosis isn't all that promising."

The air was wet and thick. My breath came in gasps. "What is the matter with you?" I struggled to my feet, gesturing wildly. "You're acting like this is a done deal, like it's over."

"It's just that I've had a while to let it sink in. A couple of weeks ago, they told us this was likely. Today was just the grand finale. Give it time."

"No, I will not give it time!" I was screaming.

"The problem is," Izzy continued philosophically,

"nobody talks about dying. I mean, let's face it, it's a bummer. I'd rather talk about Congress, or Eddie Vedder, or those sandals at Dillard's—you know, the black ones that cost about two thousand bucks?" She lay back in the sand. In the waning light, her dark hair could have been a pool of water. "We pretend we're immortal because it's easier."

"We *are* immortal, Izzy, we're juniors."

She smiled.

I tried again. "They're doing all that gene research. You could get into one of those experimental drug projects."

"Yeah, I asked my doc about it. I'm going to Miami for more tests. Maybe I'll ask there. Of course, even if I did get into one, there's no guarantee it'd work." She rolled onto her side. "But I'd like to feel . . . you know, like I'd done my part for science and all that. I would rather have found the cure for cancer myself, but hey, I'll be a guinea pig if I have to."

I dropped to my knees. The sand was already cool, but the sky still simmered with color.

"That's the only thing that pisses me off," Izzy said softly. "I wanted to do . . . well, great things."

I sat beside her. "Iz, you *are* great things already."

"You can do the great things for both of us," Izzy said. "Don't forget the twin guys in Paris, okay?"

"You are not gone. You are here. You are going to get better."

"Also, the skydiving. No, let's make the skydiving optional. The twins are enough pressure."

"I want to start this day over," I said. "I want to backspace it out of existence."

Suddenly I thought of Sam. He had been part of this day too, this day I wanted to erase. I tried to remember his quiet smile or the feel of my arms around his waist, but all I could remember was his bike flying through the air in a beautiful, deadly arc.

The moon was getting braver, taking on color and light. Izzy pointed to the spot where the turtles had hatched the summer before. "Think they'll come back?"

"They always do. Late spring they start laying, remember?"

Izzy nodded. "Think I'll see them hatch?"

"You'll see them."

"If I don't," Izzy whispered, "you can do it for me, Al. The twins, the skydiving, the turtles. Don't forget, okay? Especially the twins."

"You'll be here. You can do it yourself."

"Maybe you're right. You couldn't handle twins."

"Please, Izzy. Hope. For me. It's way too soon to stop hoping."

Izzy sat up. She shook sand out of her hair. We watched the moon trip lightly along the water. I cried softly. Izzy just hugged her knees, swaying slightly. I could feel her watching me.

"When do the turtles hatch?" she asked.

"Mid– or late summer."

"Sooner, ever?"

"Not usually."

Izzy nodded, as if she'd come to a decision. "Okay, then," she said. "Okay, Al. I'll be here."

Chapter Three

WITHIN TWENTY-FOUR HOURS, everyone at school knew about Izzy. Rumors about Iz replaced rumors about Sam. She had three weeks to live, she really had AIDS, her cancer was catching—you name it, we heard it. It was so completely horrible it was almost funny.

Izzy's parents arranged for her to have surgery at a medical center in Miami. The surgeon came highly recommended and was doing some interesting work with brain tumors, Izzy told me brightly. Iz actually seemed excited about getting to hang out at such a swell facility. She was even hoping to get a tour of their lab. I wondered if maybe she was in denial. While the rest of us were so frantic, she was . . . well, just Iz.

Wednesday, Izzy insisted on coming to school, even though she and her parents had a four P.M. flight to Miami. She had a physics test that morning she didn't want to miss. Afterward we sat under a palm tree, having lunch. Neither of us was very hungry.

"Are you nervous?" I asked her.

"Nervous? Just 'cause some stranger's going to drill a hole in my head and scoop out a handful of brain? Nah, I'm not nervous. Now, if I were having a nose job, *then* I'd be nervous."

Izzy brushed a long wisp of hair out of her eyes. When she came back from Miami, all her hair would be gone. I thought she would still look beautiful, and I told her so.

"Just promise me this, Al. If I come out of surgery a cauliflower, make them yank the plug." She tossed her lunch into the trash. "I told my parents the same thing, but you know how attached parents can get to their kids. I mean it. If I come out drooling—or if suddenly I start watching *Full House* or something—put me out of my misery."

I managed something between choking and laughter.

"No, I'm serious," she insisted. "Promise."

"I promise." I was glad we were both wearing shades. I didn't want to see her eyes.

Izzy leaned close. "Dark, brooding semistranger at three o'clock."

I followed her gaze. Sam. It was the first time I'd seen him since that afternoon in the grove. He'd probably been cutting classes again.

I hadn't even mentioned him to Izzy. Somehow

26

all those new, amazing feelings about Sam had gotten lost in all the worry about Iz.

He was leaning against the spiny trunk of a nearby palm, maybe looking at us, maybe not. He was wearing sunglasses too.

The damp breeze played with his hair.

"Bad Boy Sam," Izzy said. She pushed down her sunglasses. "You know, I kind of like the look of that guy."

"Sam?" I asked neutrally. "How come?"

"Well, when you're freakishly tall, it sort of limits your options, Al. He has the definite advantage of being over six feet." She repositioned her glasses and turned onto her side. "And he's got one of those great smiles. Like he knows some really juicy secret but he's not going to let you in on it. Plus," she added, "there's that Harley. Guaranteed to piss off Mom."

"I think his Harley is out of commission." As soon as I said the words I wanted to swallow them. This was a stupid time to bring up my infatuation with Sam. I wanted to discuss it with Izzy, but not just then, not that day of all days.

"Yeah? How do you know?"

I plucked at a piece of grass. "I saw him crash it. In that grove where I go riding. It was totaled, pretty much."

"You're kidding. Why didn't you tell me this?"

"Well . . ." I paused. "It was Monday."

"Oh." Izzy nodded. "So what happened?"

"He bled on my T-shirt."

"Very *Rescue 911*. Is that it?" She grinned. "No mouth-to-mouth? No CPR on that smooth, firm young chest?"

"Nothing life-threatening."

She cast me a questioning look. "Do I take it sparks flew?"

"No sparks, Iz," I lied. "He came, he crashed, he bled. That's it."

"Good, because I'm thinking maybe I'll just saunter on over there and ask him out. 'Hey, bay-bee, I know your Harley's dead, but maybe you could still take me for a ride.'"

"Yeah, right."

"Too much?" She shrugged. "What do I care, anyway? You know, I believe the specter of death is liberating. What's the worst that could happen? I ask him out, he says no, I die. I ask him out, he says yes, I die. Either way, the rejection part is sort of small potatoes in the grand picture, no?"

"Are you serious?"

"I don't know. I don't know anything any-more, Al."

She lay back on the grass and sighed. "You think I'll die a virgin?"

"Yeah, I'd lay odds on it. But I'm figuring you'll be about ninety."

Izzy laughed. "You're such an optimist."

"I *am* an optimist. And I wish you'd see the light and convert."

28

"I wish I could. It must be nice to assume that if you just think good thoughts and say the right things, everything will turn out peachy keen."

The edge of sarcasm hurt. "You make me sound like some New Age Marcia Brady," I said.

"Quiet, Marcia." Izzy nudged me. "Look who's limping over."

Sam was slowly making his way across the lawn. I wondered if he'd ever seen a doctor. The cut on his forehead was a thin black line. I felt this wild rush of hope as he approached. I don't know what I was hoping for, exactly. Unless maybe it was the insane fantasy that he'd swoop me into his arms and tell me that his life had been forever changed since that moment we'd first touched in the orange grove.

"Hi," he said.

So much for the fantasy.

"Hi," I said.

"I believe that would be my cue," Izzy said. She grinned. "Hi."

"You're Izzy, right? French fourth period?"

She took off her sunglasses. "Yeah," she said. "I'm surprised you remember. You're not there much."

He smiled, then fell serious. "I heard about your tumor."

It was the word, so ugly and bare, that everyone else had been studiously avoiding. Izzy wasn't fazed. "Yeah, well, I'd been meaning to get my hair cut, anyway."

29

Sam laughed, but his eyes were pained. "Life has a way of sucking sometimes," he said. "You having surgery?"

"Monday. Tests first."

"That's tough."

We settled into an awkward silence. "I hear your bike got totaled," Izzy said. "Speaking of tough."

Sam reached into his jeans pocket and retrieved a five-dollar bill. "Here," he said, looking at me for the first time. I felt my cheeks blaze. "What's that?" I asked, frowning at the bill.

"For your shirt. A down payment," Sam said.

"Please." I laughed. "It was just an old T-shirt."

He hesitated, then stuffed the bill back in his pocket.

"Well, anyway, thanks again for your help," he said.

I listened for something to hang on to—a throaty catch in his voice, eye contact that lingered just a second too long—something, anything I could take as a sign he felt the same way I did. But Sam just turned back to Izzy and took off his sunglasses. "Good luck," he said softly, and then he was limping away.

"Damn," Izzy said. "I blew my big chance."

I wondered if Izzy was serious, and if she was, what I would do about it. She was always talking that way about guys but rarely followed through. I think she felt as shy and inadequate as I did around them, which was crazy. She had a *Sassy*-cover face, an IQ in the stratosphere, and she was even, as my grandmother liked to put it, amply endowed.

Most of the time, though, Izzy was so immersed in her own little world that she didn't quite follow what was going on in the real one. A guy would flirt with her, and about four days later she'd realize it. Whereas I, on the other hand, was attuned to every nuance, every look, every word, every word implied between words. A guy would accidentally run into me in the hall and that evening I'd be picking out bridesmaids' dresses.

Izzy sighed. "Did you sense anything there between us? A sort of fatalistic bond? Or was that just pity? Who cares, I'll take what I can get. Maybe if I'm back in school in time for Valentine's Day, I could ask him to the dance. Would that be tacky?"

"No," I said, looking away. "It would be very feminist of you."

"I'm halfway serious, you realize."

"Plan on it, Iz. Definitely. It'd give you something to—"

"Don't say 'to live for.'"

"I . . . I was just going to say that it would give you something to look forward to, that's all."

"Maybe. We'll see. Do you think he likes the gangly, bald, puking type?"

"You forgot brilliant."

"If the radiation treatments make me nauseated, we can discuss quantum mechanics while I pray to the toilet."

"Is this what they call gallows humor?"

"I'm getting on your nerves, right?"

I touched her shoulder. "I just want you to think positively, okay? For me?"

"I am." Izzy jumped to her feet. "I'm thinking positively about the slinky black number I'll be able to fit into for my big date, what with not being able to keep down food. How's that?"

"It's a start," I said. I stood, brushed off my jeans, and grabbed my backpack. "Are you serious?" I asked—casually, I hoped. "About Sam?"

Izzy gave a short laugh. "What do you think?"

"I don't know. You sounded—"

"Please, you know me. I talk the talk, but I can't walk the walk. Or is it the other way around?" We fell into step together. "Besides, I've got other things to think about." A look of weariness settled over her lovely face. "Explain to me again how this optimism stuff works."

My heart was in my throat later that afternoon as I walked Izzy through the crowded halls to the lobby. Her parents were waiting stiffly in the car.

I pulled two crumpled packages out of my backpack.

"I should have known you'd make an event out of this," Izzy groaned. She signaled to her parents and we sat on the wooden bench by the door. The vice-principal, Mr. Lutz, was standing at the entrance to the administrative offices, watching us. He'd already given Izzy a big pep talk— "The

32

prayers of the school are with you," "Don't worry about falling behind," that sort of thing.

Izzy tore the shiny paper off the first present and pulled out the pair of red pajamas. "Excellent," she declared. "Although I'm sure the docs would have preferred a nice little teddy."

"I read—" I stopped myself. For the last two days I'd pulled up every article about brain cancer I could find on my computer. One had mentioned that button pj's were better for brain surgery patients—nothing to pull over your head.

"Read what?"

"Nothing. Open the envelope."

Izzy slit open the manila envelope. "For your wall at the hospital," I explained as she pulled out the Michelin street map of Paris.

She stared at the map, her index finger slowly tracing the *P* in Paris over and over.

I hugged her and we both started to cry. Izzy pulled away, scooping up the gifts, and ran out the door to her parents' waiting car.

"It'll be okay," I called, but the door had already closed, and Mr. Lutz was the only one who heard me.

Chapter Four

I WAS FUMBLING with my locker combination the next morning when Sam emerged out of the river of students surging through the hall. "Hey," he said. He had this low, reined-in voice that made you want to listen harder.

"Hey," I said brilliantly, still struggling with my lock.

"I brought you this." He passed me a rolled-up wad of gray fabric. It took me a second to realize it was a T-shirt. "I felt bad, you know, about your shirt. And I'm kind of strapped for cash until I get my bike fixed."

I unrolled the shirt. It was huge and smelled of Tide.

"It's almost new. I only wore it twice. And I washed it." Sam shrugged. "Anyway . . . I just, you know, wanted to pay you back."

I held the shirt by the shoulders. A guy's shirt, *Sam's* shirt. Preworn. I would wear it to bed until it was nothing but shreds, threads, subatomic particles of cotton.

Sam grimaced. "You're right, what a jerk." He grabbed the shirt away. "Man, what was I thinking?"

"No." I grabbed it back. "I want it. Really."

He relented. I rolled up the shirt and stuffed it in my backpack before he could change his mind.

"Thanks. Now you've more than paid me back."

He hesitated. "You hear anything about your friend?"

"Izzy? She called me from her hotel last night. They're doing lots of tests, then she gets admitted Sunday for surgery Monday. She'll be fine." I nodded, convincing myself. "Izzy's tough."

"I hope so."

"Well," I said, displaying more of my verbal virtuosity.

"I guess I'll see you around, then." He shrugged. It was a shy little-boy gesture, but his smile was more knowing. I sensed he was waiting for something, but what?

Before I could decide, he was gone.

I opened my backpack and stared at the shirt. A shudder of guilt went through me. I was playing tug-of-war over a T-shirt while Izzy was lying in an exam room somewhere, being poked and prodded and scanned.

Suddenly I started to cry. I ran to the nearest bathroom and locked myself in a stall. It was stupid, my crying like that, stupid and self-indulgent, but it was all I could do for Izzy just then, and besides, I couldn't stop even if I'd wanted to.

After a long while I took out Sam's shirt. I breathed in the comforting scent of the soft gray fabric. Then, feeling like an incredible idiot, I wiped my eyes and headed for class.

The rest of the week it rained like crazy. The snowbirds down for a taste of Florida sun were devastated, but I liked it. It seemed right, under the circumstances.

Saturday afternoon I drove Sara to a friend's. Traffic on the main drag moved in fits and starts, aggravated by lost tourists and senile locals. The windows were fogged up and the defroster didn't work. We cracked the windows and the rain poured in, magnifying the wet-dog smell of the carpet.

We slowed to a creep. Bridge construction over Phillipi Creek. Sara cleared a window with her arm. "Look at that poor guy hitching," she said. "Give it up, already. Who's going to let you in their car, all soaked?"

Somehow I knew, even before I looked. It was Sam.

I concentrated on the I'M NOT A TOURIST—I LIVE HERE bumper sticker on the Honda in front of me. A huge, urgent hope filled me. It seemed to take up all the room in my body.

We came to another stop. He was ten feet up on the shoulder. Our eyes met. I closed mine and waved him in.

"What are you doing?" Sara demanded. "You can't let him in the car. They'll find us in little pieces in Oscar Scherer Park ten years from now."

"I know him. He's okay." Understatement of the millennium.

Sam opened the back door and slid in. "You seem to have this habit of rescuing me." He smiled at Sara. "I'm Sam Cody." He extended his hand. She stared at it, surprised, then shook it.

"Sara," she responded. "You know my sister?"

"Yes and no. Mostly no."

"Take my advice, go with the no."

Sam leaned forward, elbows on the back of the bench seat. He was so close. I felt impossibly dizzy. I clutched the wheel till my fingers ached.

"She saved my life," Sam confided to Sara.

Sara eyed me with new respect. The clot of traffic broke, and I stepped on the gas.

"I more or less gave him a Band-Aid," I clarified.

"She ripped off her T-shirt to bind my wounds," Sam said.

Sara gasped softly.

I shrugged. "Well, I couldn't just let him *die*." I looked in the mirror and managed to return Sam's smile. "Where are we going?"

"Kayla's," said Sara.

"No, I meant Sam."

He hesitated. "Drop me as far north as you're going."

"It's pouring. I might as well take you home, Sam."

He shook his head. "No, really."

"Let her take you home," Sara advised. "Trust me. She has no life."

I sent her my most withering look. She did not wither. She didn't even shrivel up around the edges. "Savor your last few hours on earth," I told her.

Sam leaned back. I checked the mirror. He was grinning. His T-shirt was a wet second skin. Very becoming. He winked at Sara. "Beneath that playful banter lies a deep sisterly bond, right?"

"Beneath that playful banter lies deep sisterly hatred," Sara replied. "You have any sisters?"

"Two brothers, younger. One just right for you, actually."

"Where do they go to school?"

Sam looked out the window, suddenly quiet. "They're . . . somewhere else."

"Where?" Sara persisted.

"Sara, where do I turn for Kayla's?" I interrupted.

"Bahia Vista. Duh. You've only been there, like, ten thousand times."

"I was hinting you should stop the inquisition. Duh."

"I was just asking the guy—"

"Stop asking."

She turned around, arms crossed, sending me her own version of a withering look. A few minutes later I pulled into Kayla's drive. Sara leapt out without a word, slamming the door. The window glass shuddered.

I smiled weakly. "Sibling rivalry, I guess."

"It'll pass."

"You can sit up front, if you want. The seat's premoistened."

Sam joined me. I watched Sara slip into Kayla's house. "I don't know why she hates me so much."

"It's normal."

"If my family's normal, we're all in trouble. Put on your seat belt, okay?"

"She's probably intimidated."

"Intimidated?" I asked, backing out of the drive.

"She's got this smart, beautiful—" Sam began, then paused and fumbled with his seat belt. "Uh, sister. Sure, she's going to feel intimidated."

Beautiful was not a word I'd ever heard in connection with my person. My cheeks sizzled. I lowered the window a little more, soaking my left arm.

I savored the word. Sam, this beautiful guy sitting next to me in my smelly-dog station wagon, had just called *me* beautiful.

I realized I hadn't spoken in a few aeons or so.

"Do you intimidate your brothers?" I asked quickly.

Sam laughed at some private joke. "No. No danger of that. They pretty much think I'm crazy."

I shot him a glance. "Should that worry me?"

"Probably."

I stopped at the corner. "So where to? And don't say 'wherever.' It's pouring and I'll feel like a jerk if I just let you off by the side of the road so you get even more soaked. Besides, you heard my sister. I have no life."

Sam tapped grease-stained fingers on the dash. "Okay, then. Out Clark Road, past the highway."

I nodded. We drove in silence for a while, the rain hammering. "I didn't see you yesterday at school," I said to fill the quiet. "I mean, in study hall I noticed . . ."

"I was working. At Smitty's. That garage on Route 41." He held up his hands as evidence. "That's where I was today. Trying to resuscitate a '78 Dodge. In my free time, I'm working on my bike. A guy I work with helped me dig it out."

"What about school, though?"

"What about it?"

"You know. How can you afford to miss?"

"I can't afford not to."

"But you'll—" I looked at him, and he smiled vaguely.

"I'll what?"

"Well, fall behind. Don't you read the propaganda? Your GPA will drop. You'll never graduate, your life will be over, and you'll have to spend your days working as a—"

"Mechanic?"

"No, no." I wanted to start over. "That's not what I meant at all."

I stole a glance at him. At that moment Sam looked older than I was by decades. I felt the way I had a few summers before, when all my friends had gone to camp and I'd stayed home. They'd come back changed—wiser, flushed with secrets I couldn't know. Sam made me feel like that.

The rain was giving up. Sam gave me more directions, and I turned down a quiet two-lane road. We were far out in the country, a flat expanse dotted with the occasional trailer, small ranch house, or fruit stand.

He picked up a muddy folder on the floor. "'Save the Manatees,'" he read. "Those big walrusy things?"

"This group I belong to is trying to get more sanctuaries set up."

"To save this big slug?"

"Okay, they're a little homely. But they're on the verge of extinction. Manatees are kind of slow-moving, and they keep getting hit by motorboats. Man's their only serious predator."

"That's all it takes." Sam set the pamphlet aside. "I suppose some people would point out that species are always disappearing—they always have, they always will. It's easy to be an idealist and lose sight of the big picture."

"Actually, it's not. Easy being an idealist, I mean." I smiled. "Those meetings can be pretty

41

dull. But I want to be a biologist, maybe work to protect endangered species or something."

Sam crossed his arms. "You're an interesting girl, Alison."

"No, I'm not. I'm really pretty average."

"You shouldn't say that."

"Why not? It's true."

"Because you might start believing it." He motioned. "Turn here. You can stop by the mailbox."

A battered black mailbox, tilting at a precarious angle, was perched under a scraggly pine. A hundred yards up a lumpy dirt road sat a silver trailer, smooth and round as a loaf of unbaked bread. A very old car, a dull red Cadillac convertible, sat nearby, listing slightly into a muddy ditch. Everything seemed askew. It was like looking at an off-center painting.

I felt Sam watching me. "So this is home?"

"No," he said, "but it's where I live."

"I could drive you on up."

"No," Sam said quickly. Then, more casually, "There's no place to turn around." He fingered the pamphlet on the seat. "You know, I didn't mean . . . There's nothing wrong with having ideals." He gave a self-deprecating laugh. "I'm pretty sure I used to have one or two."

"You should come to one of our meetings," I suggested.

"I don't do groups."

"That's what you said about horses. And you ended up riding."

"Desperate times, desperate measures." He stared at the pamphlet thoughtfully. A huge, blubbery manatee smiled benignly from the cover. "Maybe sometime . . ."

"What?" I tried not to sound too hopeful.

"I was just going to say that maybe sometime, you know, if you're not busy, you could show me one. A real manatee. Could be the photo isn't doing this guy justice."

"I'd like that," I said casually, in my very best imitation of a cool person.

Sam hesitated. His eyes flicked to the trailer. His jaw was clenched, as if he were trying to stop the flow of words. I gathered from his sudden frown that he was having second thoughts about our going out.

I didn't know what to say under the circumstances, so I just sat there, mute and fidgety and pretending it hadn't happened.

"I don't know, maybe that's not such a good idea," he said. He grabbed the door handle as if he couldn't wait to escape.

It had to be a world record. I'd started a relationship and been dumped in the space of five seconds.

"Well, I should be going," I said hastily, hanging on to what little dignity I had left.

"Scratch that," Sam said, and I realized he wasn't talking to me. He nodded firmly. He'd come to a decision, another one. "I can work something out," he said. "How about next weekend?"

"Next weekend?" Already we were patching things up?

"Yeah. Unless I have to work. Or, you know"—he waved vaguely—"something comes up."

"Sure." This time I really sounded noncommittal. I'd been on this ride before, after all.

"So. Good. A manatee. I'd like to see one of those suckers." He got out of the car. "Thanks again for the lift."

When he grinned at me it was strangely intimate, maybe because he wasn't that free with his smiles. His whole face changed, as if the other, intense Sam had been just a stand-in, a warm-up act for the real thing.

"Oh. Any word on Izzy?" he asked.

"Surgery day after tomorrow." I clenched the wheel. "I'm sure she'll be fine. I wish there were something I could do."

I expected him to say that she'd be fine, not to sweat it, something like that. What I might have said in the same position. But he just stared at me—through me, almost.

"You do what you can," he said, and then he strode up the muddy drive.

I watched him pick his way over the puddles. I felt a little annoyed and a lot giddy and very confused. What had just happened? I tried to sort through his words and put them in neat little piles. He wanted to go out with me, but he had real doubts about the idea. He'd asked me out, but only sort of. He was interested in me, but he had serious reservations.

Or maybe he just plain wanted to see a manatee.

Still, I reminded myself, there was the irrefutable fact that he'd called me beautiful.

I started to back down the drive, but something held my gaze. A flash of movement in the old Cadillac, white hair. Sam knelt by the driver's window. I could just make him out through a thorny tangle of shrubs. He was talking to someone inside, nodding patiently again and again. He pulled open the door and reached inside. Slowly he withdrew his arms.

I backed the car up a few feet so he'd think I was leaving. Then I waited to see who would emerge from that rusting hulk.

Seconds later, he appeared. A frail old man, his body curved like a cane. Sam's right arm was around his shoulders, and his left hand gripped the old man's.

They moved toward the trailer achingly slowly. The old man had tufts of downy silver-white hair, like Einstein on a bad hair day. And while I could not be absolutely sure, I had the uneasy feeling that perched amid all that hair was a green-and-yellow parrot.

At the entrance to the trailer Sam glanced over his shoulder, saw me still there, and grimaced. The door closed.

Maybe, I thought, it was time for me to see a good optometrist.

We had Monday off because of teacher workshops. I spent it waiting in my room, watching the clock. Izzy's surgery was scheduled for eight A.M. By two I was a nervous wreck. She'd warned me it would take a long time, but that didn't make the worrying any easier.

At three Sara peeked in my door. "Maybe her mom forgot to call you," she said. "You could call her."

I shook my head. I didn't want to call her and hear that something had gone wrong. It was better to wait with hope than to call and lose it.

"Want to shoot some hoops?" Sara asked.

"No, thanks."

Sara leaned against the doorjamb, chewing on her lower lip. I could tell she was worried. Sara adored Izzy, probably because Izzy treated her like a very short adult.

"You know," Sara said, "I could call Rosa and ask. She might know. Want me to?"

"Thanks. Maybe in a while. Let's give it another half hour."

Sara turned, then paused. "Al? Did you . . . did you pray or anything?"

"My understanding is, praying works a lot better if you're religious."

"Are we religious?"

"We're agnostics."

Sara frowned. "What's that?"

"It means we're covering our butts, just in case."

"I feel like I should have prayed."

"Did you think about Iz?"

She nodded. "All day, and practically all last night."

"That's plenty good."

She stuck around for another half hour, forgetting for a while, I suppose, that she hated me. Finally she gave up. "I'll be outside playing basketball," she said.

"Okay. I'll let you know if I hear anything."

A few minutes later the phone rang. My hand trembled as I lifted the receiver. It was Rosa.

The words whizzed and blurred, Spanish melting into English, sobs, pauses. Lauren too upset . . . some of the tumor, left a lot . . . permanent damage . . . too risky . . . don't tell . . .

"What?" I whispered. "Don't tell what?"

"We're not going to tell her," Rosa said. "Why would we tell her? We want her to be happy. She deserves to be happy for what time she has, Alison."

I thanked Rosa and put the phone down.

You do what you can do, Sam had said.

"We should have prayed," I said to no one.

Chapter Five

THEY WOULDN'T LET any of us visit Izzy. She was in intensive care for several days, and even after they moved her to a regular ward, Lauren said it would be too much of a strain. I got all her friends together and we sent her this giant get-well card with a million signatures on it.

After the first week, Lauren let Izzy talk to me on the phone now and then. She was usually foggy with painkillers, and I never knew what to say. It was like talking to someone over a bad phone connection.

One thing I didn't talk about was Sam. Not that there was much of anything to say. Since the day he'd more or less asked me out, days had melted into weeks. He was in school sporadically, three days on, two days gone. I could not imagine how he pulled it off or why he hadn't been suspended already.

When I did see him we would smile at each other in the halls like shy strangers, sometimes exchanging a "Hey, how you doing?" I began to wonder if I'd been hallucinating. Hadn't he asked me out? Hadn't he, in fact, called me beautiful?

The first week, I'd summoned up my nerve after study hall and asked him if he still wanted the grand manatee tour. Couldn't that weekend, he'd said, a lot of commitments, work and everything, sorry, really. He'd had that cramped look guys get when they know they're being jerks but just can't help themselves.

Normally I would have chewed over the rejection for months, wondering what I'd done wrong. But somehow, with Izzy far off in a hospital being zapped with radiation, it just didn't seem to matter as much.

On a bright Saturday afternoon, three weeks to the day after I'd given Sam a lift, I was in the barn with Snickers when I heard a throaty whine, like a lawn mower on steroids.

Sara came running to get me. "I'm sure you'll find this as hard to believe as I do," she said, "but there's a guy here to see you."

I put down the currycomb and wiped my sweaty forehead. "Sam?" I asked, practically choking on the name.

Sara nodded. "Are you, like, you know? Dating?" she asked incredulously.

"No. We're not, like, anything." I dropped the comb into a grooming bucket. "What did you tell him?"

"That I'd see if you could fit him into your crowded social calendar. By the way, here's a helpful dating hint: horse doo-doo is a real turnoff."

I considered changing. After all, I had just mucked out Snickers's stall. I had on my boots, an old pair of patched beige breeches, and a sleeveless formfitting blue top I'd gotten on sale.

But before I could decide one way or the other, there was Sam, striding along the side of the house toward the barn. He had on tight old jeans and a grease-smudged T-shirt. He didn't exactly look like he'd just walked out of a Gap ad himself. Still, if the pulse hammering in my throat was any indication, on him the scruffy look worked.

"Hey," he said, standing in the doorway. His tall form cast a long, slender shadow. "I guess I should have called, but I got my bike fixed. And, well, I wanted to tell someone." He hooked his thumbs in his pockets. "And you're the someone who came to mind."

"Congratulations," I said doubtfully. "How did you know where I live?"

"Phone book." He gave me that sideways grin of his.

I smiled back uneasily. Why was he there? Right then? After all that time?

"Can I go for a ride?" Sara asked.

"Mom'll love that," I said, "when I have to call her at the clinic and tell her you're roadkill."

Sam cocked his head slightly and pulled down his shades. "I'm a great driver, Alison. And I've got an extra helmet."

"I've seen you drive," I pointed out.

"That was an act of God," Sam said. "Or of Firestone, anyway."

I untied Snickers and took her back to her stall. "So?" Sara pressed, trailing me. "You going or what?"

I looked back at Sam. He was watching me, arms crossed, looking pretty sure of himself. A look that, I suddenly realized, could be very annoying in a guy.

"I thought we were going to go see some manatees a couple of weeks ago," I said, preoccupying myself with a burr in Snickers's mane.

"I'm sorry about that, really. I had some stuff come up."

Stuff. What did that mean? Where had he been all those days? "What kind of stuff?" I asked.

"Personal stuff." He hesitated. "Family."

Family. I thought of all the rumors. I pictured dark rooms fogged with cigar smoke where Mafia dons spoke in accented whispers and the *Godfather* theme played in the background.

Then I thought of that little old man, the one with the parrot perched on his head.

"Just an hour," Sam said. "I promise I'll have you back in an hour."

Sara kicked my shin. "Please, it's not like you have a lot of options, Al," she said, just loud enough to be sure Sam had heard.

"I should shower first," I said nervously, not to Sara, not to Sam, more or less to Snickers, actually.

"I just got off work," Sam said. "I'm covered with grease and sweat. We can offend each other."

"There's a pretty picture," Sara said.

I looked at Sam. "I won't ride unless you wear a helmet too."

"Fine, no problem."

I closed the stall door. "If Dad asks, tell him I went to the library with Gail and there's a buck in it for you."

"Why lie?" Sam asked.

"What? You don't have parents?" I asked. "Because you have a motorcycle and my dad hasn't grilled you for three hours about whether your intentions are honorable." I turned back to Sara. "If Mom asks, tell her the same thing and I'll give you a five."

"More for Mom?" Sam asked.

"Dad'll believe anything," Sara explained.

"Oh, and if Iz calls—she was maybe going to, this afternoon—tell her the same thing, okay?"

"Why?"

"Just do it, okay?"

"Ten for Iz. She's smarter than Mom."

"Ten?" I demanded.

"Why are you lying to Izzy, anyway? It's not like you won't tell her about *him*."

52

I brushed past her. "I don't have to explain my life to you, Sara. Just do it. You're getting more than minimum wage."

"How is Izzy?" Sam asked.

"She's having radiation and some follow-up tests. She'll be back Tuesday." I didn't tell him that the surgery hadn't been successful. I hadn't told anybody except my family. It wasn't my place.

We headed to his motorcycle in the front drive.

"Will she be okay? Alone in the house, I mean?" Sam asked as I fastened a heavy red helmet on my head.

"Sara?" It struck me as an odd question, a parent's question. "Our neighbors keep an eye on her, and my parents will be home in a few minutes. She'll be okay."

But as I threaded my arms around Sam's waist I noticed Sara leaning against the porch railing, solemn and small. I almost said, "Wait, I can't leave her behind." But I didn't.

We rode far and fast. We cut through the thick, wet afternoon air till bumps rose on my arms and I shivered against Sam's back. I closed my eyes and let my mind fill with the noise of the engine and mental pictures of Sam's bike flying through the air that hot afternoon in the grove.

I could die right here, I thought, *a mute tangle of bones in a dusty field. Another tire could blow. We could rock just an inch too far to one side and skid out. Or that semi half a mile down could veer into our path.*

It wasn't just the bike, it wasn't that I didn't really know or trust Sam. I could die anywhere—I could slip on the top from a yogurt container in the cafeteria, I could fall off Snickers while we were taking a jump. I could die. Sam might even want to, in some secret part of himself.

But Izzy really might die.

They hadn't gotten all the tumor. I'd looked it up in the same books Izzy had read, and I knew what that meant. People died when that happened. Not always, but sometimes.

We sliced around a wide curve, and the earth tugged at us. It was like a roller coaster, but without the smug certainty you'd be all right. I tried to hang on to the electric buzz in my throat. That was what thinking you might die felt like. That was what Izzy was feeling.

I tried to hang on to the feeling, but it left me. All I felt was the rush of freedom, the empty place where worry should have been. We rolled down that road and I felt like we would live forever, Sam and I, and I hated myself for feeling it.

I directed Sam to a spot off Siesta Key where manatees were known to congregate. He parked the motorcycle, and we walked to the edge of a shallow cove and settled on the grass. Sun burned on the water, baking into our shoulders.

54

"The manatees chow down on sea grasses around here," I said. "They eat something like a hundred pounds of vegetation a day. Keep an eye out. You'll see their heads bounce up. I saw a mom and her calf here the other day."

Sam nodded, staring intently at the gentle water.

"There's a lot of boat traffic, though, so don't get your hopes up," I added. "Mornings are better."

"It's too bad, the boats hitting them and all. Poor guys don't have a chance."

"Those boat jerks go tearing through here, and it slices the animals open. It's so sad. They took two orphaned calves to Sea World a couple of months ago after their mom was hit. One of them died." I scowled. "I mean, look at the sign. This is a protected area, but they still go barreling through here—" I realized I was in my eco-speech mode. "Sorry. I get sort of riled up."

Sam lay on his side. "I wish I could do that."

"What?"

"Get worked up about something. It's a gift."

I looked at him. "Are you making fun of me?"

"I'm dead serious." Sam stopped talking and pointed. "There, was that something?"

I followed his gaze. "Close, but no. That's a milk bottle. So what did you mean just then? About getting worked up?"

He smiled at me, that been–somewhere-you-haven't smile. "I admire people like you, Alison. People who think they know where they're going,

55

who want to change things, be things. It must be cool to wake up and say, 'I'm going to do *x* and *y* and *z* today and it will mean something.'"

"What's the alternative? What do you say when you wake up?"

"Well, let's see. Today I woke up and said, 'What the hell day is it, do I have to work?' Then I remembered I had the afternoon off and my bike was fixed." He took off his sunglasses. His eyes glittered like the dark water. "Then I said, 'I'm going to see Alison today. And maybe that will mean something.'"

I liked the way he said it, but it scared me a little, too. So I rolled on my back and closed my eyes and let the sun warm my lids.

"Well, what do you want to do?" I asked after a while.

"You mean when I grow up?"

"Yeah. Next year, or five years from now, or ten."

"That's a long time, Alison. I don't think that far ahead. Maybe I won't be here, who knows?"

"That's crazy. What do you care about, what are you good at?"

He didn't answer. I opened my eyes and found him grinning at me. "Sorry," he said. "Leading question."

"What *else* are you good at?" I persisted, conscious of my body, of the hot sun on my bare arms and neck, in a way I hadn't been a second before.

"Not much." He looked annoyed.

"No, name something." His indifference was annoying me back. "Everyone's good at something. You're a good mechanic, you're a good motorcycle rider—well, okay, scratch that. But you're good at math or lunch or something. Tell me you know all the words to the *Brady Bunch* theme song. Tell me you can stop a moving fan blade with your tongue. Just say *something*, Sam."

He exhaled slowly. "I suppose," he said, as if it had just occurred to him, "that I'm good at watching out for people."

"But you're not very good at watching out for yourself," I countered. "Why don't you wear a helmet? Why do you smoke? I mean, it's just . . . stupid, incredibly stupid. Do you have some kind of death wish? Or is it just a way to look cool, big bad Sam with his Harley?"

He looked genuinely surprised at the emotion in my voice. "Death wish," he repeated. "Interesting theory, but I'm not really all that complex. I have a Harley because, well, I like it and it's cheaper than a Viper." He sighed. "And as for the helmet and the cigarettes, I guess they're just bad habits."

"So why don't you quit?"

"I suppose because no one ever asked me to."

"*I'm* asking."

He smiled. It was a broad, smooth smile, the kind that curled up just a little at the edges. "Okay, then."

He was making fun of me again. "What, you're going on the straight and narrow because some perfect stranger asked you to? What about doing it for you?"

"I'm not what you'd call an interested party."

I sat up, frustrated, clutching a mound of grass. He was a mystery to me, as much a mystery now as when he'd been the object of hushed bathroom speculation.

"You are really exasperating," I said. "While I'm reforming you, why don't you stop cutting school, too?"

"I can't. Sorry."

"Why?"

"I see one, I think." He sat up too. "There, by the dock. Big, ugly, round? Like a walrus?"

"Sounds right. I don't see one, though."

He nodded. "So. I've seen a manatee."

"Did not. You were just changing the subject."

"No, I saw it. Sort of like Fred Flintstone in a wet suit. Definitely a manatee. So why is it again I should care if there are only a few left?"

"Because," I said firmly, "we are the most intelligent species on the planet. And we're the ones who are killing this one off."

"And what if it doesn't work out in the end? What if you try and you end up failing? Why do it, then?"

"Because we have to try."

"Okay, then," he said. "Okay. That I understand."

58

He surprised me then by touching my hand, warmth on warmth. We both looked off at the water, neither daring to meet the other's eyes.

We sat there for a long time like that. Holding hands, only not. The world fell still and became just us and the water and the sun. It was like that sweet stirring before a storm, when you sense something is about to change and all you can do is wait.

We looked for the manatees, but they were swimming secretly in the dark grasses, waiting for a safe moment to appear. Waiting, I suppose, as we were, to see what the world had in store for them.

Chapter Six

AFTER A WHILE we rode over to a phone booth at a Texaco. He needed to make a call, Sam explained, checking his watch.

I sat on the bike, watching him dial. He turned away from me furtively. I strained to listen. "Morgan . . ." I heard. Then ". . . police . . ." Smothered, angry sounds. "When were they there? . . . back soon. Thanks."

Police. The word sent a jolt of reality through me. The rumors resurfaced. What had I really found out about this guy, this guy whose hand I'd been holding, sort of, for the last half hour—this guy I was convinced I was falling in love with?

When Sam rejoined me his expression was flat. "Something came up. I have to take you home."

"What came up?"

He reached for his helmet. "Nothing."

"You have to take me home for nothing?"

"It's not your problem."

"Maybe if you tell me, I could help."

"It's not your problem."

It was like trying to see through lead. He was not going to let me in.

"Fine," I said. "Forget it. Take me home."

He put on his helmet, climbed on, and revved the bike. Angrily, it seemed to me, but then, it was hard to tell with a Harley.

I tapped his shoulder. "Just tell me this," I yelled. "Did you or did you not rob a Get n' Go?"

Suddenly the bike fell silent and still. He looked over his shoulder.

"What exactly is a Get n' Go?"

"No, I know. It's the witness relocation program, right? Your dad's some kind of drug kingpin and you turned state's evidence."

Behind his clear mask his grin broadened. "Where *are* you getting this?"

"School. Rumors. People talk, I listen."

"Why are you even here if that's what you think? Why did you agree to come with me? Weren't you afraid I'd drive you to the nearest 7-Eleven so we could pull a Slurpee heist, maybe zap a couple of burritos as we blasted our way out?"

"I wasn't afraid," I said, suddenly shy. "Actually, I knew you weren't any of those things."

He crossed his arms over his chest. I concentrated

on the dark hairs on his arms. "What did you base that on?" he asked.

I looked past him. "You kissed my horse and you carry pocket Kleenex."

He stared at me, shaking his head. "You are one very interesting girl, Alison," he said. "A little weird, but very interesting."

Again he revved the engine. He turned back and sat there for a long time, watching a gray Taurus rise up slowly on the garage's lift.

"Come on," he said finally, reluctantly. "There's someone I want you to meet."

When we rode up the lane to Sam's place, the old man was sitting in the driver's seat of the red Cadillac. The top was down. The parrot was sitting on his shoulder. Two petite white-haired women shared the front seat.

It wasn't until we pulled up alongside that I realized they weren't petite women. They were giant poodles.

"There you are, boy." An older woman with a thick quilt of brown wrinkles appeared in the doorway of the trailer.

Sam parked the bike. "I'll be right back," he told me.

He and the woman spoke in hushed voices. I heard the word *police* again. The old man gripped the Cadillac's steering wheel, spinning it like a captain would turn the wheel of a clipper ship. The poodles and parrot stared intently through the dirty window. I followed their eyes, but all I could see was the weedy paddock behind the trailer. Far off in the distance an old horse grazed, as dented and weary-looking as the Cadillac.

I climbed off the bike and removed my helmet.

"Nice caboose," someone said, adding a wolf whistle for full effect. A shrieky voice, not quite a man's. Not quite a woman's, either.

I spun around. No one was taking credit.

"Need a lift?"

This time it was definitely the old man. I looked to Sam for guidance, but he was deep in conversation.

I approached the driver's side slowly. The man was smaller close up, with deep, pocketed eyes the worn blue of old jeans. He was wearing a natty red bow tie and a green plaid flannel shirt that hung in drapes off his frail arms. On his head was a leather driving cap. He seemed very happy to see me.

"Nice caboose." It was the parrot, I realized, vaguely relieved.

"How far you going?" the man asked.

"Uh, well, I live on Fruitville—" I began.

"I can take you as far as Vegas. Back, Forth, make room for the lady."

He snapped his fingers and the two poodles edged closer in perfect unison. Two more dogs, sweet little muttly types, sat in the backseat. One was wearing a little straw hat.

I looked over at Sam. He was shaking the

woman's hand. He caught my eye and gave me a look that said he'd be there soon.

"Hop in, hop in, let's hit the road. You play keno?"

I went to the other door and opened it obediently. "No."

"Ah, roulette, then. Thirty-two red, that's the ticket."

I closed the door. The poodles eyed me suspiciously.

"Kiss me, mama." The parrot again.

"Sam?" I called hopefully.

The old man floored the gas pedal, despite the fact that there was no key in the ignition. He turned the wheel and leaned into the imaginary curve. Even the poodles swayed.

"Hang on, sister, let's see what this baby can do."

I don't know why, but I fastened my seat belt.

He changed direction, leaning the other way. Again, everyone swayed except me. He cast me a dirty look and I felt guilty, as if I were defying the laws of physics.

Just then Sam appeared. I sighed with relief.

"Morgan, this is Alison. Alison, this is my grandfather, Morgan."

Oblivious, Morgan swerved again. Sam grabbed the wheel. "Jane told me what happened, Morgan. You found the keys, didn't you?"

Morgan stared straight ahead. "Let's hit the road and see where it goes."

"You did hit the road," Sam said. His voice was smoothly patient. "You hit it for six miles or there-abouts."

For the first time, Morgan seemed to hear Sam. "I got her up to forty-five."

"Too bad you were in the wrong lane at the time." Sam held up a set of keys. "I hid these for a reason, Morgan. Now I'm going to have to take them out of the trailer altogether. You promised—no more joyrides."

"Nice caboose," the parrot remarked to Sam.

Sam opened the door and waited. "Let's go make some burgers, huh?"

The old man turned to me. Once again he seemed genuinely, freshly happy to see me. "You his girl?"

"Uh, well, not—"

"Kid needs one. Might as well be a monk."

He looked at Sam. "Kissed her yet?"

"Kiss me, mama," said the parrot.

"Shut up, Cha-cha," Sam said.

"She's a looker," Morgan added.

The parrot bobbed its head. "Nice—"

"Shut up," Sam said again, "or we'll be eating parrotburgers tonight."

"Take her out. Ask her to a picture, ask her to a dance, *then* kiss her," Morgan suggested. He eyed me doubtfully. "You cha-cha?"

"No, I—"

"Shame, that. Ask her anyway."

"Will you get out of the car, then, and promise not to pull this crap again?" Sam asked.

"Listen to you, in front of a lady."

Sam took a deep breath. "Alison, we'll go out sometime, okay?"

The old man rolled his eyes. "A dance, something classy."

"People don't do that kind of thing anymore, Morgan."

Morgan spun the wheel, pouting.

Sam's cheeks were tinged with pink. I thought it was very charming. "Fine. Alison, let's go to a dance, somewhere, sometime in the unspecified future."

Morgan stared at me expectantly. So did all four dogs. "Okay," I said meekly. "Sure."

Morgan got out of the car. Very slowly he came around to the other side and opened my door. When I got out, he kissed my hand. His lips were cool and dry.

Sam took his arm. "I'm going to take Alison home, Morgan," he said as he helped the old man inside. The four dogs trotted behind him.

I leaned against the warm hood. A few minutes later Sam came out. He looked . . . not embarrassed, exactly. Almost relieved.

"So," he said. "Not exactly the Get n' Go, huh?"

"He's really your grandfather?" I asked. "Where's the rest of your family?"

"Back in Detroit. I just came down to keep an eye on things for a while." He smiled. "Guess I should have warned you. He's kind of unpredictable."

"I like him. I've never had my hand kissed before. Come to think of it, I've never had a parrot come on to me either."

"He has good days and bad. Actually, today's a real good day. He's pretty lucid."

I wondered what a bad day was like. "Is he the reason you have to miss school sometimes?"

Sam nodded impassively. "Yeah. That, or sometimes work." He shrugged. "Sorry about all that dance stuff."

"That's okay. You were coerced."

He hesitated. "There is some kind of dance thing coming up, isn't there? I saw a poster, I think. Hearts or something."

"Valentine's Day."

"I can't dance," he said.

"Not even the cha–cha?"

"Still, if you wanted, and things worked out, we could . . . you know. Go. And make fun of the other people dancing."

I looked over at the trailer. Morgan was standing behind the screen door, a gray shadow. The parrot was still on his shoulder.

"I'd like that," I said, and my voice quavered only a little bit.

"Okay, then," Sam said.

"Okay."

He moved a little closer. I could see the steady throb of a vein in his temple. I could see the tiny quiver of his lower lip as he leaned toward me. I could see his pupils go wide and dark.

I closed my eyes. I didn't want to see. I wanted to feel.

"Kiss me, mama," someone said. And I did.

That night Izzy called. She was really jazzed about coming home and going right back to school. The doctors were all over her about not taking on too much too soon, but she couldn't wait. I promised her we'd go out and buy lots of cool bandannas and scarves and turbans. We considered the merits of one of those curly pink taffy wigs. Funny to us, sure, but what if no one else got the joke?

I wanted to tell her about Sam, I swear I did.

I'd been kissed only twice before, once at a beach party (hyperactive tongue, excess saliva, Blistex aftertaste) and once by a guy at science camp who'd harbored a secret crush on me (no tongue, dry lips, raspberry Bubblicious aftertaste).

But this, *this* had been a real kiss. Every time I thought about it, I got shuddery and woozy and somebody started trampolining off my stomach.

Sounds awful, I know. It wasn't.

I felt like I'd traveled somewhere I had never been before. Like I'd finally been to camp, if you know what I mean.

I should tell Izzy, I kept thinking as we talked about the dirty movies available on the hotel TV—did she dare order one?—and the tedious, terrifying mechanics of radiation therapy.

I should have told her from the start. I should have said, "Izzy, something magical happened between Sam and me that day in the grove." But I didn't, because I knew it wasn't what she wanted to hear right then.

It wasn't like I didn't know that waiting might make things worse. I'd sat through two sweaty hand-holdings, that bubble gum wisp of a kiss, and a breathy, confessional mash note before I'd gotten up the nerve to explain to the science camp guy that I was already involved. (I couldn't just say I wasn't interested, could I?) Why hadn't I just *told* him? he'd moaned. Camp was only six weeks long, and he'd wasted two and a half seducing me—all the good ones would be taken.

While Izzy went on about an orderly who'd told her he liked bald chicks, I heard a soft rap on the window by my bed. I peeled back the shade. There, just visible in a veil of orange moonlight, was Sam.

His bike was behind him. I knew he must have turned it off and wheeled it across the lawn, or else my dad would have been already cross-examining him. Sam pointed to the helmet he was obediently wearing, then took it off and grinned, a little sheepishly.

"The thing is," Izzy was saying, "this orderly is coming on to me because I'm hairless. I mean, talk about your basic sick weasel."

I laughed even as I pulled up the window. The warm, flowery air billowed the shade. Sam put his hand to the screen. I put my hand over his. It fit inside it nicely.

"What a jerk," I said into the receiver.

"Hi," Sam whispered.

"Hi," I mouthed back.

"I just wanted to see you before I went to sleep," he said. We stood there like that for long seconds. Our fingers were separated by the cool mesh screen, but I could still feel the heat of his palm.

After a while he put on his helmet, turned his bike around, and wheeled it silently across the lawn.

I thought about how he'd said he was good at watching out for people. And I thought my instincts had been right, very right, that day in the grove.

"Guys," Izzy said. "Sometimes I wonder if I'll ever find one. Especially now."

"You will," I said softly.

"You think?" Izzy sighed.

"We both will," I said, watching as Sam slipped away into the warm, black night.

Chapter Seven

I DECIDED TO have a welcome-back nonparty for Iz. Nonparty because her aunt was adamant that we hooligans not cause her to overdo anything. I liked Rosa, but I think she felt I was a bad influence on her niece. Rosa was devoutly religious, and she knew my family spent Sunday mornings with the *New York Times* crossword puzzle, David Brinkley on the tube, and a bag of warm turnovers from Publix bakery. Izzy didn't go to church either, but I think Rosa held me responsible. Once I heard Izzy try to explain to Rosa that she did belong to a religion, one called science. The next day, Rosa gave her a neatly wrapped little box with a rosary inside. Apparently she hadn't gotten the message. Or maybe she had.

Izzy was due to arrive on Tuesday afternoon. After school a bunch of us rode over to the condo on Siesta Key, loaded down with balloons, crepe paper, and dorky hats. I'd invited Sam to come. He said he had to check on Morgan, then he'd see. It seemed like a natural way to ease him into the picture, just one guy among many, a casual friend, "Oh, by the way, Izzy, remember Sam?"

Somebody turned on the CD player, loud Pearl Jam to blast away our anxieties about what we would say to Iz and how we would say it. Rosa, a heavy woman in her forties, hovered in the corner like a nervous shadow. She'd lived with Izzy's family since leaving Cuba, and although she had a full-time job as an administrator at a nursing home, she seemed to me to be as much a permanent fixture in the condo as the baby grand in the living room.

"Like the balloons, Rosa?" asked Gail, one of Izzy's former teammates on the girls' basketball team. Izzy had quit a year earlier to spend more time on her science projects.

"Very nice, yes," Rosa said, not convincingly. She eyed the silver sentiments: Get Well Soon, Welcome Back, Atta Girl. There was also a Beavis and Butt-head balloon, sentiment-free.

"Nothing was quite right," I explained as I tied a balloon to a chair.

"Yes," Rosa agreed, black eyes flitting over our disruptive flurry.

"Hats, everyone," added Carla, another basketball friend who topped six-one.

Steve, Izzy's physics partner of the freckled, sincere, platonic variety, climbed onto the piano bench to hang crepe paper. "I thought about shaving my head," he said, accepting a pink paper hat from Carla. "You know, in solidarity with Iz. I've heard of people doing that."

"Izzy would think that was truly insane," I said.

"Really," Gail agreed, "she'd die if we—" She swallowed her sentence, aghast. "I mean, I meant—"

For some reason our multiple gazes pivoted toward Rosa, who abruptly left the room.

"It's okay, Gail," I said. "Face it. We're going to say and do stupid things. Izzy's cool. She'll understand."

"God, I'm so afraid I'm going to blow this. I want her to feel comfortable," Carla said.

"Well, that's not going to happen if we're all being weird," I pointed out as I went to answer the door.

I was surprised to see Sam standing there, helmet under his arm. He had a handful of limp yellow daisies ensconced in a newspaper cone. "For Izzy," he explained. "We have that field out back."

"Come on in," I said. As I reached for the flowers our fingers touched. A sweet, shuddery warmth made its way down my spine. Amazing, I thought, that the briefest touch could spin such magic.

I led him down the hall. "Everybody," I said,

73

my voice pitched a little higher than usual, "you all know Sam?"

This time all eyes pivoted to me. The looks varied from surprise to outright shock.

"That's Gail, Carla . . . well, you can figure out the rest," I said. "Let me put these in some water."

I left Sam defenseless and took the flowers to the kitchen. Gail scurried in behind me. "How do you know *him*?" she demanded.

"We've talked a few times."

"I heard he's Alec Baldwin's illegitimate son."

"I thought it was Mick Jagger." I found a tall glass and filled it with water.

"Cute," Gail said, chewing on a bright red thumbnail. "Tall and cute. Did I mention cute? Are you . . . sniffing each other out?"

"How subtle." I arranged the daisies, the warm stems already droopy. Then I lied. "No."

I don't know why I didn't say yes. Gail was a good friend. But Izzy was my best friend, and if I told Gail anything before I told Izzy, it might get back to Izzy, complicating things. And then she would think I was being patronizing, not telling her about Sam because I didn't think she was up to it. Even if that was true, I didn't want Izzy to think it. I wanted her to feel that nothing had changed, despite the fact that everything had.

We heard a commotion at the front door. Izzy's dad, Miguel, came in first, carrying a big stuffed cat and a large suitcase. Lauren followed, shepherding Izzy through the hall.

"All right, Rosa!" Izzy cried, embracing her aunt. "A keg party!"

"Isabella," Rosa whispered, sobbing hugely.

We were all staring while trying not to. Izzy looked the same, only not. She was wearing a blue bandanna tied artfully around her head, a T-shirt and embroidered vest, jeans. But there were glossy blue-black circles under her eyes, and her skin was pale and slack, like a balloon that's been blown up and deflated.

Izzy got passed around the group and hugged uncertainly, the way you do when you greet someone with a lingering case of the flu. When she got to me, we both laughed, then started to cry, then laughed again. "Check it out," I said lightly, pointing to the dining room table. "We brought munchies."

"You made Rice Krispies bars!"

"Isabella," Lauren said, "you need to go easy. You've been back on solid food for only a week."

"I ate half a pint of Chunky Monkey for lunch," Izzy pointed out. As she dove for the table she noticed Sam for the first time. "Well, well," she said, wiggling her brows, "what have we here?"

"Alison invited me," Sam explained. "I, uh, brought you some daisies. She put them in the kitchen, I think."

"How sweet." She grabbed a Rice Krispies bar

and held up her index finger. "Don't go away. I shall return."

Izzy veered into the kitchen, pulling me along. "Thanks," she said, examining the daisies.

"For what?"

"The party hats, the balloons, the . . . guests."

"Oh, well, actually—"

"Tell me the truth," she interrupted. "I look like something the lunch ladies would serve up, right? Izzy Surprise. Izzy Noodle Casserole—"

"You look beautiful, as usual, you jerk. Just a little tired."

"My mom's driving me insane. She keeps treating me like I'm going to fall over dead in the next five minutes. I'm surprised Rosa doesn't have a priest on call to give me the last rites."

"Everybody'll settle down. Give it a few days. You'll be old news."

Izzy tugged at the knot in her bandanna. "Wanna see?" she whispered.

I nodded, because I knew she wanted me to.

It wasn't the baldness that shocked me, it was the ugly truth of the dark red incision. Until that moment, Izzy's disease had been an abstraction. All of a sudden it was real. I made myself look at it the way she had to look at it every morning in the mirror.

"Gross, huh? Sorry. Bad idea." She retied her scarf.

"No, really," I said quickly. "You look like . . .

76

sort of like a white Shaquille O'Neal. With boobs."

Izzy laughed. "God, I missed you. I knew you'd treat me like me." She leaned down to sniff Sam's already-wilting daisies. "I hope this isn't an omen," she said, cupping a drooping flower. "Sweet, though, wasn't it?"

"Very."

"It was brilliant of you to invite him, Al. I need a diversion. I've been thinking I need a hobby, anyway. I was going to take up stamp collecting, but maybe I'll collect guys instead." Izzy peered down the hall. "Ah, there's a fine-looking specimen now." She glanced back at me. "Has Sam said anything useful? Like, you know, he's always had a hankering for sick chicks?"

"Actually . . ." I searched for words and couldn't find any. "Actually, he's asked about you several times," I said. It was the truth, at least.

"Close enough. Wish me luck."

I watched her race off. Lauren came into the kitchen. Her short, dark hair was flat and shapeless, her tailored navy dress wrinkled. She wasn't her usual elegant self. She draped an arm around me. "Thanks, Alison, for this. She needed a pick-me-up."

"She looks good," I said.

Lauren chewed on her lower lip, where her coral lipstick was smudged and flaked. She motioned for me to follow her to the master bedroom. As we walked down the hall I noticed Izzy talking to Sam. Briefly she touched his arm, leaning close.

The pristine bedroom was very tropical, with wicker furniture and a colorful spread. I stood by the large windows overlooking the gray-blue Gulf.

"She hasn't asked. Isn't that odd?" Lauren's voice was a whisper. "I was ready to lie after the surgery, but she never asked. The doctor came in and said everything looked good, they had done what they could, and she left it at that. I was so relieved. It was so . . ."

"Not like Izzy."

"Yes." She came over, squeezed my shoulder. "You understand, right? That we're telling everyone they got it all, and everything's going to be fine."

"I understand."

There was a soft knock. Miguel entered the room and closed the door behind him. He was tall, like Iz. She had gotten her dark, thickly lashed eyes from him. "You told Alison?" he asked.

Lauren nodded.

"We want every moment to be happy, you see," he said to me, but also to himself, I think. "That's the right thing. It is."

"Of course it is," Lauren said crisply.

I heard Izzy's melodic, up-the-scale laugh from all the way down the hall.

"What good would there be in telling her the truth?" Miguel asked.

"What if she figures it out herself?" I asked

gently. "You know how Izzy is. She can't let things alone. She'll be digging through medical textbooks again and will be on the Internet all night. What if she already suspects?"

Lauren rubbed her eyes. She leaned close to me. Her fingers tightened on my shoulder. I could feel her nails through my shirt; I could smell her perfume, the Chanel Izzy sometimes borrowed when her mom wasn't looking.

"She has only two or three months, Alison," she whispered. She pulled away, and I could see in the intense heat of her eyes that there were no tears left. "Maybe less, they don't know. The tumor was more advanced than they'd expected. For that little time, we can make it work. We can make her happy."

Miguel took my hand and we stood there silently, staring out at the water. Laughter floated from the living room. An old Stones song boomed from the CD player. I held on to Izzy's parents and they held on to me. I knew they were wondering why I, someone else's daughter, should live and theirs should not.

"I'm sorry," I said, because it was all I could say, and because I was wondering the very same thing.

The next day Izzy went back to school. After a while we started to get the hang of being around a person with cancer. Turns out it's just like being around a person without cancer.

79

That is, unless you know her prognosis and she doesn't. Or maybe she does, but you're afraid to ask and she doesn't seem to be in any hurry to bring it up.

It wasn't like Iz was in denial or anything. We talked lots about how scary everything had been and what a general pain in the butt being sick was. But it was general scariness, not specific I-might-die scariness.

I tried to get her to ventilate; I wanted to be there if she wanted to talk. I tried like crazy to sense what she wanted me to say and do, but mostly she seemed to want to go back to being just plain Izzy.

I still hadn't gotten around to telling her about Sam. I wanted to, I tried a dozen times, but she seemed so infatuated with him after the party, I just didn't have the heart to hurt her. Who cared if he'd kissed me or if we were going to the Valentine's Day dance? Making a big production out of it seemed so small-minded, so irrelevant, in the face of everything Izzy was going through.

On Thursday evening I'd just gotten off the phone with Izzy when the phone rang again. It was Sam.

"I just wanted to make sure we're still on for that dance thing Saturday," he said. I could hear the shyness in his voice, and it made me smile.

"Looks like you're stuck," I said. "I already bought a dress."

"Good. That's good. I . . . I'm glad you didn't change your mind. Morgan kind of forced you into it."

I lay back on my bed, twisting the phone cord around my finger. There was something very mysterious about talking to a guy on the phone, I decided. It was all imagination, no eyes, no lips, no gestures. All voice. I could have listened to Sam's voice all night. It had a soft urgency, like the wind parting the palms by my window, like that brief miracle of a kiss we'd shared.

"How is Morgan?" I asked.

"Not so great. We're having a rough week. But it'll be cool. I've got it all under control. My neighbor Jane is going to keep an eye on him Saturday night." He paused. "Well . . ."

"I should hang up," I said. "I've been on the phone all night with Izzy. I'm starting to feel like I'm glued to the receiver."

"She seems pretty good, under the circumstances. She going to the dance?"

I tried to ignore the hollow spot in my chest. "No. I wish she were." I cleared my throat. "I guess Izzy's so gorgeous she kind of scares guys off."

"That's too bad. She's a great girl."

There was a pause. "I should go," I said again, although I didn't want to.

"Good night," Sam said softly, so softly I could barely hear him.

I hung up the phone and sighed. I had to tell her. I knew I had to tell her.

By the time Friday rolled around I was frantic. The Valentine's Day dance was the next night.

Lunchtime, I decided. I would bring it up casually, a throwaway remark: "By the way—you won't believe this, Iz, it's got to be some kind of miracle—but I'm going to the dance with Sam. No, really, it's no big deal. . . ."

That day the honor society was selling carnations in the lunchroom to would-be romantic types. A white carnation signified friendship, pink was liking, red was all-out lust. Girls sent them to guys, guys to girls, and all day long they were delivered to classes by members of the honor society.

"I hate all this Hallmark schmaltz," Izzy commented at lunch. She sighed. "So how come nobody sends me anything?"

"Maybe because you hate all this Hallmark schmaltz."

Izzy grinned. She was wearing a Marlins baseball cap that day. I thought she looked a little paler than usual.

"I'm getting some more juice. Want some?" I asked.

Izzy shook her head. "You know, the Valentine's Day dance is tomorrow. Remember how I was going to ask Sam? Whatever happened to that?"

I stood and grabbed my wallet. *Say it, Alison.*

"I guess I lost my nerve," Izzy continued. "Do you think he was flirting with me at the party? Or was that just pity? He borrowed my French notes yesterday, did I tell you? Talk about the blind leading the blind. He's missed more school than I have. I wonder what the deal is?"

"Be right back," I said, retreating.

Tell her, you idiot, tell her, I scolded myself. Standing there in the stewed-cabbage stench of the lunchroom, it all seemed so obvious. I may have had good intentions originally, but now those good intentions were just going to make things a whole lot worse.

I paid for my cranberry juice and was making my way back down the aisle when I noticed Sam. Sam's back, actually. He was standing at the carnation table, bent over, writing on one of the little cards they attached to the flowers. Next to him stood Steve, Izzy's physics partner, all earnest concentration.

For me? I thought for a split second, then, *Please, no.* That wasn't how I wanted Izzy to find out.

I rejoined Izzy. She was checking her reflection in a knife. "Is it just me, or do I have a little bit of a Morticia thing going here with the white face?"

"Pinch your cheeks," I advised.

"Check it out." Izzy nudged me. "Sam and Steve at the flower table, did you see?"

I glanced over my shoulder and shrugged, nicely indifferent.

"I briefly entertained the notion that Sam was buying something for me, but I don't think conjugating *aller* makes for a real commitment. Do you?"

"You never know. Aren't you going to eat your cake?"

"Not hungry. Steve's there, too. He's probably buying my traditional white carnation. We send each other one every year so we don't feel left out."

"Maybe there's more to Steve than meets the eye," I suggested.

"Steve? No way. We're just good buds, you know that."

"You sure? He has a pet name for you."

"Dumbo is not a pet name. It's a term of ridicule."

"Still—"

"Nah. I've tried to look at him that way, but I can tell it would be like NutraSweet love. You know—you convince yourself it's okay, then there's this weird aftertaste." She nodded toward the carnation table. "Now, with Sam over there, it's a different story. Look out, he's coming."

"Who?" I asked, knowing.

"Sam the man." She turned and waved.

Sam smiled as he approached, a nice, generic, collective smile that encompassed us both. He handed Izzy a gray notebook.

"Thanks," he said. "You saved my butt."

"I can't think of a butt I'd rather . . . Oh, never mind," Izzy said with laugh. "I just can't pull off the Mae-West-meets-Madonna thing." She pulled back a chair. "Join us?"

"I've gotta get going," I said quickly, standing. It was way too easy to imagine where this conversation could lead. "I've got to clean out my locker."

"Me too," Sam said.

"What? Are we having an inspection?" Izzy asked.

"No, I meant I have to go," Sam said. "As in off campus."

"Cutting class again?" Izzy chided.

"I've got a reputation to uphold. I've already had a nice heart-to-heart with Lutz about my unexcused absences."

"Well," I said. "Gotta go."

"I'll walk out with you," Sam offered.

"Give me a sec, I'll come too," Izzy said.

"No," I said quickly. "When I said go, I meant, you know—go." I pointed to the rest room in the corner.

Izzy looked at Sam hopefully. "You could keep me company while I don't eat my cake," she suggested.

"Sure," Sam said, giving me a confused glance. "For a minute. Then I gotta get moving."

I beat a quick retreat to the bathroom. I stayed in there a long time, long enough to talk myself yet again into doing what I knew I had to do. I would explain the whole thing to Izzy, how I'd wanted to protect her, how it hadn't worked out exactly the way I'd planned.

I gathered up my books and was just about to leave when the door burst open, nearly flattening two sophomores lavishing attention on a shared Marlboro. Izzy stood in the doorway. She held up a huge bouquet of red carnations triumphantly.

"Read the card!" she screeched. "Read it nice and slow, so I can take in the exquisite poetry of it all."

She handed me the little card with a Xeroxed heart and arrow on the cover, courtesy of the art department.

Love, Sam.

I looked up at Izzy's deliriously happy face.

"'Love, Sam,'" I read.

"Say it again."

"'Love,'" I said, extra slowly, "'Sam.'"

It was one of those pictures that lock into your mental photo album forever. Izzy, in a cloud of Marlboro smoke, her baseball cap just a little crooked, the bouquet cradled in her arms like a newborn. Smiling in a way that told you she'd forgotten, for that blissful, impossible moment, about being sick.

"You sure it says 'love'?" she asked.

"It says 'love,'" I confirmed.

"It was so sweet! He walked away, very casual, and I was throwing my lunch in the recyclables bin, and all of a sudden this guy from the flower table comes over and says, 'Weren't you sitting over there a minute ago?' And I say yeah, and he says, 'These are for you.' And when I got done peeing my pants, I read the card, and then I looked all over for him, but he was gone. Too shy to stick around, isn't that cute?"

I closed my eyes, then opened them. Izzy was still standing there, clutching the bouquet. What was going on? *Why had Sam done this?*

"It's a miracle," Izzy said. Her eyes glowed feverishly. Tiny beads of perspiration covered her upper lip.

I gave her a hug. The sweet-bitter smell of the flowers, crushed between us, filled the smoky air.

"'Love, Sam,'" she said, amazed. And then her smile went flat and her eyes rolled back in her head and she slipped through my arms to the floor.

Chapter Eight

AFTER THE SCHOOL nurse and the crowds and the ambulance and the chaos, I ran to the phone in the lobby to call my mom and see if she'd drive me to the hospital. The ambulance guys had told me there was no way I could go with them. And I'd taken the bus to school that day so the car could have some carburetor work done. I was struggling to retrieve a quarter from my backpack when someone touched my shoulder.

"What happened?" Sam asked.

"I thought you were gone already," I said, too frantic to think about the flowers he'd sent Iz.

"I was just pulling out when I saw the ambulance. Some guy in the parking lot told me it was Izzy."

"She passed out. Damn it, I always have tons of change in my purse—"

"I could take you to the hospital."

"Good, yes, that would be good," I said.

I kept seeing her blank face, which had been the thin blue-white color of skim milk. "Her cap fell off," I said shakily. "You could see that awful scar. I made them put it back on her head before they took her out."

Sam reached for my arm, and we hurried down the hall. We were almost out the door when I heard someone call my name. A hall monitor, I figured, but it was a stubby, nervous freshman carrying one white carnation.

"Are you Dumbo?" he asked.

"What? No, that's my friend."

He thrust the carnation at me. "Could you give this to her? We're, like, totally screwed up on deliveries."

I scanned the card. It was from Steve.

"Another secret admirer?" Sam asked as we headed out to his motorcycle.

I put on my helmet. "What do you mean, another?"

Sam looked a little hurt. "The . . . you know. The flowers."

It took me a second, but it finally clicked.

They'd switched the flowers. Duh.

"Damn," I said. "That's all Izzy needs."

Then I felt something awful: relief. The flowers had been for me after all. And I was glad.

"A simple thanks will do," Sam said.

"Thanks," I said. "But why couldn't you have put my name on the front of the card?"

"What's wrong, Alison?"

"It's not your fault, Sam. It's mine. Let's go see Izzy, okay?"

As we rode to the hospital all I could think of was Izzy's gloriously happy face as she'd clutched that bouquet.

How could I ever, ever tell her the truth now?

Lauren and Miguel were already there by the time we arrived. "She's fine," Lauren said. "Just too much too soon, and a reaction to the medicines she's taking. I knew I shouldn't have let her go back to school."

"She insisted," Miguel reminded her.

"Can we see her?" I asked, breathing in the smells of disinfectant and sickness.

"They're moving her to an upstairs room," Miguel said. "You can see her there. Room 402, I think. We're going to talk to the doctors, then we'll be right up."

"But stay for just a minute," Lauren said. She gazed at the white carnation I was still holding, then at Sam. "You're Sam, right? We met at the party."

He nodded.

"She said something about some flowers you . . . It was nice, it meant a lot to her. Thanks."

"Actually—" Sam began, but I tugged on his arm.

90

"We'll see you upstairs, okay?" I said quickly.

By the time we were out of earshot he was shaking his head. "They screwed up the flowers, didn't they? Since you were right there in the lunchroom when I bought them, that guy said, 'Hey, don't worry about it, I'll just walk them on over now.' But then Steve came over, and I have a feeling things got messed up."

"Look," I said, "just play along, okay? She was so thrilled, Sam. You should have seen her face."

"But they were for you."

"I know." I touched his shoulder. "I'm glad."

We headed toward the lobby, a cheery area painted in primary colors. "I'm going to call my mom and tell her what happened and that I'll be here for a while. Can I bum a quarter?"

Sam fished in his jeans pocket. "Here. Alison, I can't just let Izzy think I'm interested in her—"

I held up a finger, then called the clinic and told Janet, the receptionist, what had happened. Sam leaned against the wall, arms crossed over his chest, looking distracted and a little annoyed.

Just as I hung up, Steve and Gail bolted into the lobby. "She's upstairs," I said. "She's okay, just a reaction to her medication."

"Thank God," Gail said.

"Who's the flower from?" Steve asked as we herded into the elevator.

"Flower? Oh. You." I thrust the carnation at Steve.

91

"Misdelivered. They're as bad as the post office."

When we got to the fourth floor I pulled Sam aside. "I know it doesn't make a lot of sense, but trust me, okay? If Izzy brings up the flowers, just go along with it. Shrug and say 'Aw, shucks' or something."

"I don't think that's a good idea, Alison. She'll get the wrong picture."

"I know that. But this is the wrong time to give her the right picture. You didn't see her lying there on the floor, Sam."

Sam stared at the ceiling.

"Look, she's bald, she's got a mile-long gash in her head, she just passed out, and to top it all off, she had the tuna supreme at lunch. Give the girl a break."

He grinned reluctantly. "I'm a lousy liar."

"Yeah, but you're good at keeping your mouth shut, and that's the next-best thing."

"You are one very interesting girl, Alison," he said. "A little weird, but very interesting." He reached over and gently caressed my cheek. I wanted to kiss him, but instead I made myself move away.

Izzy was sitting up in bed, with Steve and Gail on either side. She looked pale in her yellow-bunnied hospital gown, but otherwise unscathed. "Well, well, the gang's all here," she said.

Steve thrust the carnation at her. "It got side-tracked," he explained.

Izzy read the card, laughed, and gave him a hug. She smiled shyly at Sam. "And speaking of flowers . . ."

Sam looked at me for guidance. "Yeah, well—"

"You have to admit, fainting was a bit of an overreaction, Iz," I said quickly.

"Time out. What am I missing here?" Gail asked.

Lauren and Miguel entered. "Okay, enough socializing," Lauren scolded.

"Bye," Izzy said reluctantly. "Next time I'll try to time it better. Maybe faint during an English test."

As we filed out Izzy grabbed Sam's hand. I pretended not to notice, leaving him to fend for himself.

I said good-bye to everyone else and waited in the hall for Sam.

"What did she say?" I asked when he emerged.

He cast me a worried look. "She said she felt the same way," he said.

"What did you say?"

"I said, 'Take care.'"

"Good, good, this is good."

Sam shook his head. "Let's go. We need to talk."

I gave Sam directions to Turtle Beach. It was still nice and hot, and we sat on the sand and let the water play over our bare feet. Sam was very quiet, which was good, because it gave me time to

93

fine-tune an idea that was percolating in my brain.

"A lot of loggerhead turtles nest around here," I said at last. "Izzy and I monitored a nest up there late last spring. The mother turtle comes from thousands of miles away to the beach where she was born. She lays her eggs, and then when they hatch about sixty days later, the baby turtles head straight for the water. It's incredible to watch." I paused. "This year, Izzy may not . . . she may be, you know, too sick."

Sam scooped up a handful of sand and let it rain down softly on my toes. "Alison, you can't let Izzy believe something that isn't true. It isn't right—not for her, not for any of us."

"Just hear me out," I said. "What if you—just for a little while, I mean; you don't have to marry her—what if you *pretended* you were interested in Iz, maybe went out with her a few times? It's not like it would take a lot of acting skill, Sam. After all, she's funny and brilliant—did you know she was a Westinghouse semifinalist? And you have to admit, she is beautiful."

"Well, she's no *you*."

I laughed. "Yeah, she's the beautiful swan, and I'm more, say, gerbilesque."

Sam abandoned the sand. He moved closer to me, so close I could feel his warm breath on my cheek. "You are beautiful, Alison, just for the record. Izzy is too, in a different way. But don't ask me to lie to her. I can't. It's not right."

I watched a young couple walk arm in arm down the wet brown sand. "Have you ever been in love, Sam?"

He wrapped his fingers in my hair, and an electric tingle traveled the length of my spine. "Funny you should ask," he whispered. "As a matter of fact, I think I am right now."

I let myself savor the sweetness of the words. Then I fixed my gaze on Sam. "Well, Izzy never has," I said. "I don't know why. Maybe she intimidates guys, who knows."

Sam trailed his fingers down my arm. "I don't want to know about Izzy. I want to know about Alison."

"Funny you should ask," I said softly.

Sam took my face in his hands.

"Wait, Sam. Wait. I have to tell you something. It's about Izzy." I felt my voice losing power. I didn't want to say it out loud because that would make it real. "She's going to die, Sam. Soon. She has only a couple of months. And she doesn't . . . her parents won't tell her."

Sam pulled away and stared out at the water. "I'm sorry, Alison," he whispered. "I'm really sorry."

"All I'm asking is that you spend some time with her. Get to know her. She's so great. And she deserves to know what it's like to really care about someone. She'd know what it was like to have a boyfriend . . . and I know she likes you."

I was crying. *Damn*, I thought. I didn't want to cry because I wasn't sure why I was doing it. I wanted to know it was for Izzy and not for me.

"Izzy deserves better," Sam said. "She deserves more than a stand-in."

"She does," I replied, my voice hoarse. "She deserves to go to college and win a Nobel prize and have kids and travel the world and grow old. But that's not going to happen, is it?"

Sam took in a long breath. "Why are you really doing this?"

"Because . . . because she's my best friend and I love her and she's dying."

"So you're willing to give up whatever it is that's going on between us?"

"I don't want to give you up," I said. "I just want to share you for a while."

Sam stared at me. His gaze was flat and impenetrable. "That's not how it works, Alison."

Before I could answer, Sam was already striding across the beach. The soft sand filled in each footstep as quickly as he left it, as if he'd never really been there at all.

When Sam dropped me off at my house, I eased inside the front door and paused in the hallway. I didn't really want to talk to anyone if I could avoid it. The air was filled with the garlicky tang of my dad's tomato sauce, and I could hear him in the kitchen, singing along (badly) with his favorite Grateful Dead CD. Loudly too, which explained why they hadn't heard Sam's bike.

Sara was in her bedroom, bouncing her basketball off the wall, a habit my mother had long since given up trying to break.

In the living room, my mom was sitting back on her heels, wiping up a semichewed pile of something that vaguely resembled a slipper of hers. Strands of hair had escaped from her blond braid and fell in wisps around her face.

"I clean up dog vomit all day, Jim," she was saying. "I am a veterinarian. I live and breathe dog vomit. All I am saying is, we have too many pets."

"Just a dog, a cat, and a horse," my dad called from the kitchen. He danced (badly) into the living room, a wooden spoon in one hand. "Man, you're one gorgeous hunk of woman," he said to my mom.

She held up a piece of paper towel. "I am scraping dog vomit off your fifteen-year-old carpet with the cat pee stain we have to cover with your mother's sewing basket, and you are actually capable of having impure thoughts?"

My father bent down to kiss her, then let her taste the tomato sauce.

"More garlic," she said.

"No way."

"Way."

It was like an old, reliable sitcom I'd watched a

thousand times, my very own *Gilligan's Island*. Every day I would tune in and they would still be there, my father and mother and Sara, doing silly, normal, boring things. That's what I'd always thought, anyway. But I'd always thought Izzy would be there forever too.

"Hi, guys." I stepped out of the shadows.

"Alison, honey, how's Izzy doing?" my mom asked. She tossed her cleaning supplies aside and sat with me on the couch.

"She's okay. A reaction to the medicine, mostly."

"I called Lauren at the hospital. She said Izzy'd be out by tomorrow."

"We sent her some balloons," my dad added. "Corny, but we figured it was more upbeat than flowers."

"Thanks, Dad."

"I've got sauce simmering," he said. "Dinner in fifteen minutes." He touched my hair. "You okay, sweetie?"

"I'm okay."

My mom put her arm around me and we sat there, side by side. I leaned my head on her shoulder and tried to remember how it felt when I believed she could fix everything.

Bogey, our aging Labrador mix, sauntered in and casually nosed the site of his crime. He jumped on the couch and draped himself over our laps.

"We have too many animals," my mom said.

She sniffled and I realized she was crying. "Damn. I didn't know what to say to Lauren. What do you say to someone who's watching her daughter die?" She grabbed a piece of paper towel and wiped her eyes. "How're you doing with this, baby?"

"It doesn't feel real," I said. "Izzy's there at school with me, and nothing's changed except she doesn't have any hair. That's how it should be. I mean, I don't want to treat her any differently. I want everything to be just the same, because I think that's what she wants." I scratched Bogey's ear, considering. "But . . . there's this guy."

"Sam, of the Harley."

"You know?"

"I doubled your money to Sara."

"Why didn't you ask me about him? You were supposed to freak about the Harley. That's the whole point, Mom."

"Your dad did. But I gave *him* ten bucks." She stroked my hair. "I knew you'd get around to telling me sooner or later. Besides, I once had a dark, mysterious man who rode a motorcycle."

"Really?"

"Yeah, but your dad sold it for a VW Beetle."

I smiled, for the first time in what seemed like decades. "The thing is, I want Sam to date Izzy."

"Ah, the plot thickens. And how does Sam feel about this?"

"I think maybe he thinks I'm insane. I also think maybe he thinks he loves me."

"And is this reciprocal?"

I hesitated. "It doesn't matter. This is about Izzy. She likes Sam too. I think she could like him a lot. And I thought maybe if they dated for a while . . ."

"Alison, it's not quite that simple. Maybe," my mom said gently, "you need to think about why you're doing this."

"For Izzy. Who's dying. That part *is* simple."

"You know, just because she's sick, hon, it doesn't mean you have to put your life on hold. Just because something bad's happened to Izzy doesn't mean you can't have good things happen to you. You think she'd want that?"

"This isn't about guilt."

"Maybe not just guilt." She sighed. "Love is scary sometimes."

My father reappeared, still brandishing a spoon. Tomato sauce striped his cheek like war paint.

"I rest my case," my mom whispered. "Scary stuff, love."

"Who's in love?" my dad asked.

"No one," I said, sliding out from under Bogey. "Not me, not Izzy, no one's in love."

"Try my sauce?" my dad asked. "It's new and improved."

"I don't think so, Dad."

He looked a little disappointed.

"Alison," my mom said. "Just be there for Izzy. And we'll be there for you, okay?"

"Thanks, Mom. I'm going to go clean up."
I paused in the hall. "Dad?" I called.
"Yeah, kiddo?"
"Trust me on this," I said with a weary smile. "It needs more garlic. It always needs more garlic."

Chapter Nine

THE CARBURETOR IN the station wagon was fixed, so I was drafted to take Sara over to a basketball scrimmage at her elementary school Saturday morning. As she climbed into the front seat, wearing her baseball cap, I suddenly thought of Izzy. If sickness could happen to Izzy, it could happen to anyone—to Sara, even. It seemed I could not look at the world anymore without seeing it through the dark lens of Izzy's illness. If it was hard for the rest of us, I wondered how Izzy managed to get through the day.

We stopped at McDonald's on the way. "Do you think Mom and Dad will ever die?" Sara asked between sips of her chocolate shake.

"Statistically, it's pretty likely," I said lightly.

She studied her straw, frowning.

"Not for a long time, though, Sara. We're talking half a century, easy, okay?"

"That's not always how it works," she said.

"No. But usually." I could see her working it through, toying with the question as if it were a painful scab. She looked so trusting and untested. Had I ever thought about these things at her age?

"It's hard, huh?" I said. "Izzy and all."

She nodded, chewing on a fry.

"What are you thinking?" I asked.

"How old I would be in half a century. Sixty." She seemed relieved. "Sixty. That's really old."

I smiled. "Ancient. Petrified, practically."

"Okay, then," she said, brightening. She handed me a fry, and for some reason I felt a little better too.

We had just passed the sign for Jungle Gardens, one of those mini-attractions with grayish alligators and tired bird acts, when Sara pointed to a figure on horseback up ahead, moving sluggishly along the shoulder of the busy road.

"That's gotta be an act from the show," she said.

"He shouldn't be out here in this traffic," I said.

"He's got a parrot on his head. What else could it be?"

I put on the brakes. Ahead of us, other cars slowed too, eyeing the little figure on the aging nag as the two meandered through a Jiffy Lube lot.

"And there are dogs with him," Sara continued.

A cop car ahead of us pulled into the Jiffy Lube. "You think they'll arrest him?" Sara asked. "I mean, it's not like it's a crime to be weird in this country, is it? Poor old guy, he looks lost."

"He is lost." I pulled into the lot next to the Jiffy Lube.

"Why are we stopping? I'll be late."

"The man on the horse. He's sort of a friend of mine."

I parked the car. The cops were already approaching Morgan, waving their arms. He saluted back.

"You know that guy?" Sara asked.

"Yeah." I sighed and pulled the keys from the ignition. "We went to Vegas once."

It took a while, a long while, but I got everything worked out. I called Sam at his job and he came over right away. The police were very nice. After all, the state was loaded with little old people who didn't know where they were going.

I volunteered to ride Clementine, Morgan's horse, home, and the cops drove Morgan back to his trailer. Sara had her choice—cop car or motorcycle ride with Sam. No contest. She climbed on the bike and hugged Sam gingerly, as if she were holding an expensive, very breakable vase on loan. Then she gave me a victorious grin and they roared off together.

When I got to Morgan's trailer I found Sara and Morgan sitting on the front steps, talking animatedly. Sam was sitting in the Cadillac, the top down, sipping a Coke, his eyes somewhere else.

"Once again, Alison to the rescue," he said as we clomped up.

"Well, technically, I'm supposed to ride up on a white steed." I dismounted and stroked the horse's mane. "How old is this gal, anyway?"

"Very. Morgan used to own a ranch in New Mexico. That was after a stint as a logger in Oregon. And his bouncer-in-Vegas phase."

I glanced at the old man. I felt certain that if a stiff breeze came up he'd dissolve in the wind like a dandelion puff.

"*Morgan* was a bouncer?" I asked.

"At a casino."

"Al! Watch this!" Sara called. The parrot was on her shoulder. She whistled, and the pack of dogs surrounded her. A clap, a twist of her hand, and all four did a simultaneous backflip.

I blinked in disbelief.

"Oh, yeah," Sam said. "I forgot the part where he trained animals for the Ringling Brothers circus."

"You're not kidding."

Sam smiled slowly. "Nope. Morgan's had quite a life."

"Is that how he ended up here, in Sarasota?" The city had been the winter home of the circus for many years.

"Yeah, he had a lot of friends here. They're dead now, mostly. Or gone."

"The little dogs ride on the big ones' backs, too," Sara called. "And the poodles can ride Clementine."

"Not right now," I said. "She's had a tough

day. She needs to be cooled down, then hayed and watered."

"I'll do it," Sara said. "Okay, Morgan?"

Morgan nodded vaguely. He looked impossibly tired, but very content.

"I can't believe Morgan was able to ride that far," I said softly. "To tell you the truth, I can't even believe he managed to climb on."

"It varies," Sam said. "Sometimes he's perfectly coherent, some days he doesn't know his own name. He'll lie in bed for a week at a time, then he'll get full of energy and pull some stunt like this."

He glanced over at Morgan and a look passed between them.

Sam's jaw tensed.

I gave Clementine to Sara and went over to Morgan.

"Well," I said. "Quite an adventure, eh? You must be tired."

"I am," he said. "A little."

"How about a nap?"

"Poker after that?"

"We'll see. Come on." I held out my arm and he took it.

Inside, the trailer was dark and tidy. There was a small bed, a couch, an ancient and very tiny gas stove, a TV set with an aluminum foil antenna. I led him to the bed in the corner. He lay down obediently but with a hint of distaste, like a tired little kid conceding naptime. I covered him with the old handmade quilt at the foot of the bed.

"Morgan?" I asked. "Where were you going today?"

He worked his mouth, looking past me. "I guess," he said, "I never thought to ask."

"I was just curious."

He closed his eyes. "Tonight we'll go to Vegas. Or else Wisconsin."

"Either one would be fine," I said, but he was already asleep.

The sun was blinding after the shadowy trailer. I joined Sam in the car.

"He didn't used to be that way," Sam told me, running his finger around the nubbed rim of the wheel. "It's just the past year or so that he's changed. He was always so—" he looked up at the sky, as if he could find the words there, "so much more *real* than anyone else I knew."

I reclined my seat and let the sun melt me into it. "You must have seen him a lot when you were a kid, huh? My grandparents are all up north."

"It wasn't like that, exactly." Sam turned in his seat. "Hey, you want some lunch or something? I owe you."

"No, thanks. I kind of like just sitting here."

"I'll take you back to get your car whenever you want."

"No rush. Sara's having a blast with the greatest show on earth over there. She was supposed to go to a basketball game, but I think the bike ride with you trumped it big time." I closed my eyes. "Morgan told me we were going to Vegas tonight. That, or Wisconsin."

"He lived in both of those places. And a hundred others," Sam said. "I'd go see him every summer, sometimes during the school year too. Didn't matter where he was." He shook his head. "Once I spent four weeks with him on a shrimp boat in the Gulf."

"How old were you?"

"Seven. It was great. I decided I was meant to be a pirate. Turned out I was allergic to seafood."

"I can't believe your mom let you go."

"She didn't let me go. She sent me."

I sat up just as Sam reclined his own seat. "She sent you? Your mom sent you away to a shrimp boat when you were seven?"

Sam closed his eyes. "She sent me all kinds of places, me and my two brothers."

"Did she send you here, too?"

Sam shook his head. "No, this I did all on my own. She thinks I'm slightly crazy, coming down here."

"I don't understand."

He didn't reply. I leaned on my elbow, watching him. His cheeks and arms were reddened by the sun. With his eyes closed, he looked younger, more vulnerable.

He reached out for my hand. I hesitated, then I

took it, and he held on tightly. His eyes were still closed, his other arm was back behind his head, his feet were up on the dash. He might have been taking an afternoon nap, except for the way he squeezed my hand.

"When I was growing up," Sam said, "it wasn't all that good. My mom and dad fought. A lot. They were pros at it. When summer rolled around, my mom would ship us off to wherever my grandfather was. My grandmother died when she was still young, and my grandfather was kind of footloose, but I suppose my mom thought it would give us kids some breathing room. In her own weird way, she was trying to do us a favor." He sighed. "When I was nine or so, my dad split for good. For years my mom swore he was coming back; it was pretty pathetic. I always liked Morgan for that. I'd ask him if my dad was coming back and he'd say that was about as likely as pigs flying."

"Well, your mom . . . she was probably trying to protect you."

Sam opened his eyes. "Sometimes it's better just to hear the truth and get it over with, Alison. Anyway, my mom kind of lost it for a while—a nervous breakdown, I guess you'd say. They were all set to stash us in foster homes, but Morgan showed up right as they were packing our bags, literally." He laughed ruefully. "Talk about your white knight. He took care of us till my mom got better. After that he moved around some more, and then he ended up here."

Sara ran through the field, flanked by the dogs. Watching her, we both smiled. "So why did you come down here?" I asked. "You said your mom didn't want you to."

"Morgan took a Greyhound up to Detroit for a visit this last Christmas. A neighbor took care of the animals. Only problem was, he ended up in Kalamazoo, not Detroit. I mean, he was really out of it. So my mom started thinking that maybe it was time to put him in a home. But when she mentioned it Morgan went ballistic. Mostly because he couldn't bear to leave the animals, but also, I think, because he knew it meant . . . you know, the beginning of the end. I mean, those homes will kill you. My mom didn't want to do it, it really tore her up, but there didn't seem to be any alternative. Until—"

"Until you decided to come down and look out for Morgan yourself," I said.

"Well, that's the idea, anyway. Mom's worried I can't handle him, but I had to try. Morgan was always there for me when I needed him."

Sam let go of my hand. He sat up and rubbed his eyes, staring at the trailer affectionately. "I just want to . . . you know, keep an eye on things. Not forever, I know it can't last forever, but for a while longer. If I can just keep Morgan under control, I know I can make it work. My mom's sending me money, and I've got my job, and Morgan had a little cash saved up. . . ."

"But you're missing so much school, Sam. And

110

the police today, and Morgan taking the car out—"

"I know." He clutched the wheel. "Believe me, I know." He reached into his jeans pocket and handed me a folded letter. "From the vice-principal. One more unexcused absence and I'm history."

"They can't do that."

"Actually, Lutz has been pretty cool. He knew the situation going in, and he and the teachers have cut me a lot of slack."

"I think . . . I think what you did, coming down here to take care of him, was really sweet."

"Yeah, I'm one sweet guy," Sam said. He looked at me, his eyes damp. "If only you'd known him before, Alison. I mean, he just loved life so much. Nothing scared him. He was so free." He scowled. "Those homes are like cages. When my mom brought it up, it was the only time I'd ever seen Morgan cry."

He dropped his head onto the wheel. "God, you must be thinking I'm insane."

"I don't think that at all," I said. "I think it's wonderful, what you're trying to do."

He turned his head toward me, still leaning on the wheel. He looked so hopeful, it hurt to see it.

"There's this neighbor, Jane. The one you saw here the other day? Her husband had Alzheimer's, so she knows what it's like. And she's really fond of Morgan. Sometimes she comes over and keeps an eye on him for me. I think that if I can just work out the scheduling, I can pull this off. I can't be

111

with him all the time, obviously. But I'll do the best I can. I just have to make him understand that this will work only if he's on his best behavior."

"I could help," I offered. "I could come over sometimes, when you're working."

"No," he said firmly. "I can't drag you into this too."

"I like Morgan," I said. "He told me I have a nice caboose."

"That was his parrot. Although it's true. Thanks for offering, though." Sam cocked his head. "What are you smiling at?"

"I was just thinking . . . I'd heard all those rumors about you, and I'd considered all sorts of bizarre possibilities. This one never occurred to me, though."

"You think I'm demented."

"Actually, I think you're amazing. In a demented sort of way."

Sam leaned toward me. He cupped my face in his hands, gazing at me as if he were seeing me for the first time. The barest breeze rustled the grass. After a moment he let go and we sat there silently, watching as Sara marched the dogs across the field.

"I'm sorry," Sam said suddenly.

"About what?"

"Izzy and all that. I want to help. I just . . . I couldn't pretend that way."

"It was probably dumb. Demented, you might even say."

"Not demented. Noble." Sam grinned, but I

could tell he was serious. "Altruistic."

I thought about my mom's words the day before. "Not so noble."

"What do you mean?"

"Maybe there's a tiny amount of guilt mixed in."

"What kind of guilt?"

I shifted uncomfortably. "Part of it is that it seems wrong to have something good happen to me right now. You know, when something so bad is happening to someone I care about."

"And the other part?"

"Never mind. I'll sound like I'm twelve."

Sam smiled knowingly.

"Okay, guilt, as in . . ." I hesitated. "As in I liked you from the day we met, but then only a few hours after that, Izzy said she liked you, and I didn't want to bring it up because she'd just found out about being sick." I came up for air.

"You liked me."

"Yes." *I love you,* I added silently.

"And now you're willing to give me up for the good of mankind."

"No. For the good of Izzy." I opened the door. "Look, I should get back to my car," I said. "I'll go get Sara."

Sam drummed his fingers on the wheel. I could see he was working his way to a decision about something.

"Alison," he said at last, "I have bad feelings about this. I think it's a mistake. Not for you and me, but for Izzy." He paused briefly, then added, "Whatever we do, we have to make sure we don't hurt her."

Suddenly I realized what he was saying. I felt a strange, combustible mixture of elation and defeat.

"Of course we have to make sure we don't hurt her," I said softly.

"You're still convinced this is a good idea?"

"She likes you, Sam. Just go out with her, have fun, let her have a boyfriend for a little while. It's only . . ." I struggled for a gentle word. "It's only temporary."

"Temporary," he whispered.

We gazed at each other silently, realizing what that meant.

"So," Sam said at last. "I guess this means the dance is off, huh?"

"You can't dance, anyway. Besides, if we went, the word would get out, and Izzy would be bound to hear about it."

Sam got out of the car. He came to me, took my hand, and pulled me close. "You do realize I'm in love with you, right?"

He kissed me then, an urgent, long kiss, and I let myself forget about everything, everything in the world.

Even Izzy.

Sam pulled away. He looked at me, pure concentration. "Now that we've got that out of the way, you can give me Izzy's number."

Chapter Ten

B Y THURSDAY IZZY was back in school, acting as if nothing had happened, as though she'd fainted just for the extra attention. We spent our lunch period in the library, sneaking Doritos while I helped her catch up on her missed homework.

"So what did the doctor say yesterday?" I whispered.

Izzy looked up from her notebook. "You know how doctors are. They don't actually *say* anything. They just mumble pompously." She adjusted her scarf, a silky green number that made her look very old-Hollywood. "He and my mom did a lot of conferring. I think the consensus was I'd go to school no matter what they said, so they'd better just shut up and let me go."

"How much more radiation?"

"Just another week, probably—three more times."

"That's good, huh? You won't be so tired then."

"Yeah, it does kind of wear you out. But I'm not getting nauseated or anything, which is a definite plus." The glass door to the library opened and Izzy nudged me, instantly switching gears. "Sam! Oh, God, and I'm wearing my Joan Crawford scarf. I wish I had my Marlins cap."

Sam wandered the floor, scanning the stacks. Beneath the table I actually crossed my fingers.

Izzy yanked a blush compact from her purse and flipped it open. "You know, I haven't heard a word from him since the hospital. I'll bet it scared him off."

"He's not around much," I pointed out, grabbing another Dorito.

"No, it's the hospital thing. Although I was wearing that sexy backless gown with the bunnies on it." She closed the compact with a sigh. "I should call him over. No, that looks so desperate. On the other hand, I *am* desperate."

"No, you're not."

"Yes, I am. I'm hairless. Hairless equals desperate."

Sam wandered behind Izzy and caught my eye. He gave me a frantic look, like a cornered animal. I averted my eyes. No way was I going to blow this by letting Izzy catch on.

"He's looking this way," I said.

Izzy studied her physics book. "Which means he's looking at you."

"My face or your rear, what do *you* think?"

Izzy half-snorted a laugh, then tried to compose

herself. "Your face is every bit as lovely as my butt, Al," she assured me. "Is he coming this way?"

"Yeah. He looks a little nauseated. That's good."

"Nauseated is good."

"It could be pre-asking-out nausea."

"Oh, God, oh, God, please," Izzy whispered, then groaned. "Listen to me. I'm talking to a deity I don't even believe in."

I kicked her gently. Sam was closing in. "I think you're supposed to do all the questions at the end of chapter seven," I said loudly.

"Ladies," Sam said, straddling a chair, "you are in possession of contraband in the form of high-fat snack food."

"Hey, it's our first offense," Izzy argued.

"You can buy my silence with a couple of Doritos," Sam said. His eyes bounced off mine for a split second. "Or you can go out with me tomorrow night."

Izzy's pale cheeks colored. "You drive a hard bargain. Just don't put this on my permanent record."

"Okay, then." Sam wiped his palms on his jeans. "Sevenish. I know where you live. We'll . . . I don't know. Have a snack-food orgy. You know I have a motorcycle?"

"I can't wait to tell Mom."

"Don't forget your extra helmet," I said, instantly regretting it.

"How do you know he has an extra helmet?" Izzy asked.

The edges of Sam's mouth curled ever so slightly. I knew what that look meant—*I told you this wouldn't work.*

"That time in the field where he nearly killed himself—remember I told you about it? He had one then. I found it in a ditch."

I smiled back at Sam. He stood up abruptly. "I'll see you tomorrow night," he said to Izzy.

"Sooner," Izzy said.

"Hmm? Oh, yeah. French."

As he left he brushed my shoulder with his arm. No big contact, not a major foul, but instinctively I pulled away.

Izzy watched him go, perfectly serene. But as soon as he was out of sight she threw her fist in the air. "Yes!" she cried. "We have liftoff. Doesn't he have the most incredible you-could-crawl-into-them eyes?"

"Excellent eyes."

"And those kind of Christian Slater lips, with that sort of Tom Cruise nose."

"Excellent assorted body parts."

She looked so ecstatic. I felt a sweet rush of power, like any successful matchmaker, but it was more than that. I felt positively generous. Almost, as Sam had put it, noble.

"God, I'm being a ditz, aren't I?"

"Izzy, he's gorgeous. He's sweet. He sent you

flowers. And you're going out. What's not to ditz over?"

"What makes you think he's sweet?"

"I'm an excellent judge of character."

"I'm not, though."

"Sure you are," I said.

"Remember the last guy I had a crush on? Jerry? Tall, very-tall-so-he-must-be-perfect-for-me Jerry? Remember how we had lunch outside by the flagpole? And how he said he had something to share with me? Do you remember what he shared?"

"Yes, Iz. I remember."

"Say it."

"No, Iz. I will not say it."

"Say it."

"I don't remember."

"He blew milk through his nose, didn't he, Al?"

I tried very hard not to smile.

Izzy dropped her head to the table. "Oh, man, what if he's another Jerry?"

"He's not," I said confidently.

"What if he doesn't like me?"

"He will," I said, but just to be on the safe side, I resorted to the crossed fingers once again.

That afternoon in study hall I wrote Sam a simple, no-nonsense, I-just-want-to-help note. Things were getting off to such a good start that I wanted to make sure they stayed that way. I kept imagining a last-minute crisis with Morgan interrupting the plan, Sam calling Izzy with some bogus excuse, Izzy devastated.

I folded the note and passed it back.

Sam,
    Izzy's so psyched!!! You should have seen her. I know you guys will have a great time. Need any help with Morgan? I'd be happy to keep him company. Honest.

Al

A few minutes later my note was returned. Sam had written at the bottom in a nearly illegible scrawl:

A—Thanks, no. Jane volunteered to keep an eye on him. Had a talk with M, he's promised to behave, all's well.
    Glad Izzy's glad.
    I still love you.

I still love you.
I read the words a thousand times, but I did not turn around. I crumpled up the note, then reconsidered, folding it neatly and tucking it into my notebook. When the bell rang and we shuffled toward the door, Sam and I ended up right next to each other. We walked side by side, as stiff and self-conscious as a bride and groom heading down the aisle.

When we reached the door we went our separate ways without a word.

That night Sam called me. "Are you sure about this?" he asked me yet again.

"I'm sure."

"Do you think she knows?"

"No," I said. "I'm sure she doesn't. And it has to stay that way."

"I love you, Alison," Sam said.

I waited. I could hear the breeze nudging the palms outside my window, I could hear Sam's even, steady breaths.

"I love you too," I said, and then I hung up the phone.

On Friday afternoon Gail and I went over to Izzy's for the great pre-date conference. Most of it was spent on what Izzy called her very own personal Easter parade: a steady procession of headwear.

She was very cool about letting us see her head. Part of it was red from the radiation she'd been receiving, as if she'd been sunburned. The technicians had marked her scalp with purple ink to make it easier for them to pinpoint her treatments.

We settled at last on a black scarf. I advised against a skirt (the motorcycle again), so she opted for a pair of black jeans with a great vest Rosa had embroidered for her.

121

"We have to go, Izzy," I told her a few minutes before Sam was due to arrive. "We have empty, dateless lives to lead."

"Stay," she pleaded. "Stay till he gets here."

"No," I said.

"Let's," Gail argued. "We can live vicariously."

"Come on, Gail." I pulled on her arm urgently.

Izzy led us to the door.

"You look great," I told her.

"Gorgeous," Gail agreed. "Our little Isabella, all growed up."

"Do you know where you're going?" I asked.

"Not a clue," Izzy said. She grinned. "You know what's great about this? I feel normal for the first time in ages. You know, healthy normal. For the first time I'm not thinking about radiation and doctors and tumor size. Well," she added wryly, "at least I wasn't until now, when I brought up how I wasn't thinking about it. The *point* is, all I care about at this particular second is me and Sam."

That was all I needed to hear to know that Sam and I were doing the right thing. Whatever else happened, Izzy would always have this moment when, for a fragile bubble of time, she was just another nervous girl getting ready for a first date.

That evening I was lying in bed reading when Izzy called. "How was it?" I asked as soon as I grabbed the phone, knowing it was her.

"Perfect." Her voice was tipsy with emotion.

"Perfect guy, perfect date, perfect, perfect, perfect."

"No first-date nerves?"

"No, that's the amazing thing. Sam's just so gentle and funny and sweet. Not at all what we thought, the whole mysterious tough-guy thing."

"No awkward long pauses or anything?"

"No. We went to Caragiulo's for pizza and it was like we'd known each other forever. He was so cool about my being sick—really open, not like most people. You know how they freeze up."

I twisted the cord around my finger. "Did you find out much about him?"

"Not much. A little. He told me he's from Michigan, and he's staying with his grandfather. That's about it. He talked about you a lot, though."

"Me?"

"Yeah. I didn't realize you two knew each other that well."

"Well . . ." I hesitated. "We have study hall together."

"That's what he said. Anyway, he thinks you're pretty cool." She paused and laughed softly. "Of course, *I'm* the one he kissed."

I tried not to think about what that felt like, letting go into that sweet rush of feeling when his lips had touched mine. "And?"

"Perfect. Just . . . so . . . perfect. I need a new word. Something that transcends *perfect*."

"I'm glad, Iz. I'm really glad."

"You know what's great? I may still die a virgin,

123

but at least I won't be sixteen and never been kissed."

Die. That word, so casual.

"How can you tell when someone's, you know, really right for you, do you think?" Izzy asked.

"It's just like in the movies. Tight head shot and the music swells. If you're really meant for each other, the camera fades away discreetly."

She laughed. "Well, I should go. Rosa's afraid I've overdone it. I come home, she feels my head and instantly makes me take my temp. So it's, like, some minute amount over normal and now she's stuffing all kinds of rude Cuban concoctions down me. OJ and pig livers or something."

"I'm so glad you had a good time, Iz. You deserve someone like Sam."

"Hey, Al? Thanks."

"For what?"

"For hooking us up."

"I didn't . . . what are you talking about?"

"You know, inviting him to the party, giving me the moral support so I wouldn't chicken out on the date."

"All in the line of duty," I said softly. "What are friends for?"

I hung up the phone and went to my dresser. As I took off the soft gray T-shirt I was wearing and put on another one, I began to cry in hard, hurting gasps.

Tears flowing, I folded Sam's shirt up neatly and

put it in the bottom drawer under a pile of clothes. Out of sight, where I'd forget I'd ever had it. Where I'd forget the uneasy whispers of regret that had made it so hard for me to hear the joy in my best friend's voice.

Chapter Eleven

FOUR WEEKS PASSED. I saw Izzy less because she saw Sam more. She thought she was falling in love. I told her I thought she deserved it.

She was getting sicker, you could see that. Already there had been a couple of seizures, both at home. Her right leg sometimes dragged a bit when she walked. Occasionally she slurred her words just the tiniest bit. But despite the headaches, the steady weight loss, and the terrible fatigue, in a strange, bizarre way, I don't think I'd ever seen her happier. She was always laughing, always trying to stay in high gear, almost as if she was trying to milk every precious moment.

Sometimes I thought I saw a ragged edge to all the manic moments, like watching an actress fall momentarily out of character. But I chided myself when I thought those things. Was I looking for a snag in her happiness, a sign all wasn't well in the relationship I'd fostered?

I hoped not. I hoped I was letting go of Sam, sharing him the way I'd promised myself I would. Freely, out of love for Izzy, no questions asked. There would be time enough for Sam and me. We had all the time in the world. Izzy didn't.

After a while I got used to seeing Izzy and Sam whispering, holding hands, doing the things people falling for each other do. He and I never talked, unless it was in Izzy's presence. He didn't even acknowledge me in the halls. It was as if, having switched his attentions to Izzy, Sam couldn't deal with me on any level, not even as a friend. After their first date he'd taken me aside in the hall to explain that he had to keep his distance from me. It was too hard, he'd said, too complicated otherwise.

It hurt. I have to admit it hurt in a way I'd never hurt before, a dull, empty ache that never went away. But it was nothing, nothing like the pain I knew Izzy was silently enduring. That's all I had to remember when I saw Sam's long fingers tangle with hers, or watched him kiss her so tenderly I'd wonder if he'd ever really cared for me at all.

At times like that I would feel the awful hot-steel burn of jealousy. But then I would look at the black half-moons under Izzy's eyes and her sweet, off-kilter baseball cap, and I would wonder what kind of horrible person lived inside me that I could even feel such a thing.

One time, soon after Sam and Izzy started dating, a bunch of us were in the lunchroom together. I was sitting next to Izzy. She said something that made us all laugh, and all of a sudden, Sam leaned forward to kiss her. He cradled her face in his hands and kissed her long and slow while we all watched, a little embarrassed, a little fascinated.

While he was kissing her he opened his eyes and looked right at me. I didn't know what I saw in his eyes at that moment—hurt? anger?—but I knew I didn't like it. And I knew I didn't like the acid grip of regret and jealousy I felt, looking at them together. I'd stopped feeling noble. At that moment I just felt angry.

I got up to leave before the kiss ended. I was halfway across the lunchroom by the time Izzy could call out to me. I slipped out the door as fast as I could, pretending not to hear.

Late one afternoon I was working on an English essay when I heard a familiar noise slice the air. I looked out my window and saw Sam talking to Sara in the driveway. My mom tapped on my door.

"Al?"

"I heard."

She peered inside. "Shall I tell him you're coming?"

I stared at my notebook. "Tell him I'm not here, okay?"

She gave me that disappointed look that mothers have a patent on.

"Don't," I said.

"What?" All innocence.

"Look at me that way. That superior mother-knows-best way. This is working, Izzy is totally in love with Sam, I do not have anything to say to him, end of story."

She joined me on the bed. "What if Sam's not in love with Izzy? What if this isn't working, and that's what Sam wants to tell you? Whatever happens, you don't want Iz to be hurt, now, do you?"

I sighed. "Fine. I'll talk to him in the driveway. But do me a favor and don't invite him to dinner, okay?"

"I would never humiliate you that way. We're having leftover goulash."

I checked the mirror. I looked like . . . well, like leftover goulash. Not that it mattered.

"What's up?" I said when I reached the porch. Sara was sitting on Sam's motorcycle, doing her best Evel Knievel impersonation.

Sam hooked his thumbs in his pockets. "I wondered if we could talk."

"I've got that English thing due tomorrow. I'm kind of swamped."

"A few minutes, that's all. I was just over at Izzy's."

"She's okay?" I asked in alarm.

"She's okay. Real tired. She's having more trouble with her right side. But you know Iz. She's pretending everything's fine." He locked eyes with me. "Me, I'm not so good at that."

"I don't think we want to have this talk."

"I don't think we have a choice."

Without a word I turned, held open the screen door for him, and led him into the house. "Sam, Mom. Mom, Sam."

"Hi . . . I guess it's Dr. Chapman, right?" Sam said, extending his hand.

"I'm flexible," my mom said. "I'm sorry Alison's dad isn't here to meet you, Sam. He used to own a Harley himself."

Sam looked impressed.

"Don't think he's cool. He sold it for a VW." I gestured toward the porch. "Come on. We can talk out back." I sent my mom a look meant to ensure total privacy.

We sat on the patio furniture in the backyard, face to face, a white plastic table separating us. "Alison," Sam said without preamble, "I miss you."

"I miss you too, Sam," I said, struggling to sound neutral.

"At first I was just hurt and really angry with you for suggesting the whole thing with Izzy. But after a while the hurt started to go away and I realized I just plain missed being able to talk to you."

"So why have you been avoiding me?"

Sam rubbed his temples. "Because it's too much, it's too confusing."

I tapped my fingers on the table. "Izzy's in love with you, you know."

"I know. But I'm still not sure this is a good idea."

"Why not?"

"Because I . . ." Sam rolled his head back and closed his eyes. "Because this is all getting so complicated. Because I miss you."

"This isn't about us right now."

"I feel like Izzy deserves the whole truth," Sam said. "Whatever that is."

"Why do you have to make this harder? It's working. It's working fine."

He leaned forward, studying me. "I don't know how to say this, Alison."

"Your feelings for me don't matter right now," I interrupted, paving the way to the place I knew he was going. "There'll be time enough—"

"You don't understand. I do still have feelings for you." He gave a wry smile. "Major feelings. But that's not the problem. The problem is, I'm . . . I guess I'm starting to have feelings for Izzy too."

He looked at me for absolution. I could see the pain in his face. I could hear it in his voice.

I didn't react. I didn't want him to know that at that moment I wanted to take everything back. Hearing him say the words out loud, I realized that I didn't want him to love Izzy. At least not the same way he loved me . . . the way I'd thought he loved me. I wanted him back. For myself. Suddenly I didn't want to share him anymore.

I don't think I've ever hated myself as much as I did at that moment.

I reached for his hand and squeezed it. "But this is good, this is great," I said, forcing lightness into my voice. "This is what I *thought* might happen. Of course you're falling for Izzy. She's beautiful and brilliant and hey, she's my best friend. I've got good taste when it comes to friends." I laughed brightly. "This is good, Sam. God, don't fight it."

"This isn't what I wanted to happen. I wanted you."

"It's okay, Sam. Really."

Sam pounded his fist on the table. It rocked back and forth on the cement porch. "I'm not like you," he said, jumping to his feet. "I like things nice and simple. I love you. I want to be with you. I know we're trying to do what's best for Izzy and I know she's a great girl and I know it's natural I would be attracted to her, but damn it, Alison, it was supposed to be you and me. And you've managed to make it messy and complicated and impossible."

I watched him pace past me. *It isn't me,* I thought. Sam was the one who was making things impossible.

"Maybe that's how love is," I said. "Maybe it's always messy. I don't know."

"What about Izzy?" Sam asked. "I mean, here we are, all tiptoeing around her like she's an imbecile, pretending she's just got a hangnail. In the meantime, she's practically picking out wedding dresses. Don't you think maybe she deserves the whole truth about you and me?"

I clenched my fists. "I don't see the dishonesty. You honestly have feelings for Izzy. Fine. And no one's told her she's cured or that she's going to live forever. No one's lied about that. So what's so wrong with letting her be happy for a little bit?"

"It's wrong if *you* can't be happy. Eventually she'll sense it, eventually she'll know you resent her and she won't quite know why. Or—or I'll be kissing her and thinking of you or something, and it'll be like one of those bad movies where you blurt out the wrong name."

"Or maybe you'll just be kissing her and thinking of her," I said calmly. "Maybe that's what you're afraid of." It was my turn to stand. "I won't resent Izzy eventually, Sam, because this was my choice. Besides, there is no eventually. Eventually implies time. And Izzy doesn't have any."

"And what about when she . . . if she . . ."

"Shut up. This is ghoulish, it's horrible."

"What if I fall in love with her, Alison?" Sam whispered.

"Then maybe you weren't ever really in love with me."

Sam spun on his heel and headed for the side yard, taking long, fast strides. I followed him to the driveway. Sara was still sitting on the bike.

"How's Morgan?" she asked.

"He's okay. He had a lot of fun with you that day."

"Maybe we could come by sometime."

"Maybe." Sam put on his helmet, and Sara relinquished the bike to him.

"Is he really all right?" I asked.

Sam looked at me sharply. "We've had a lot of talks, he's promised to behave. It's cool."

"Izzy told me there'd been some problem with him wandering off again."

"I said everything's fine." Sam started the bike, and the air vibrated with sound.

"If you need any help—"

"I don't think so."

Sam nodded at Sara and took off in a blur of noise. She watched him go, head cocked, squinting as he vanished down the road.

"I don't get it," she said.

"What?"

"I don't get you and him and Izzy."

"I told you, Sara. He likes Izzy now."

"But I thought he liked you." She had the look of someone who knew she was being lied to, but couldn't quite figure out how.

"It's complicated, Sara." I sat on the front steps. "You reach this point in your life and then, *bam,* everything's really complicated. Sometimes I wish I could have stayed your age forever."

"Ten isn't so great. Ten pretty much sucks. You might as well be invisible." She grabbed her basketball, which was wedged under a bush, and began to dribble. "You think maybe sometime we could go see

Morgan and the animals again?" she asked casually.

"Someday, maybe. But not right away."

Sara dribbled faster, making a tight circle on the driveway. "Al, I've got this game coming up soon, a big tournament." Her voice was neutral. "Can you come? On a Saturday morning?"

"Sure."

"Really?"

"Of course, Sara."

"You want to play some ball?"

"I don't think so. I've got an essay to finish." I headed for the door.

"Al?" Sara called. She stopped dribbling.

"Yep?"

"How come we can't go back to see Morgan?"

"It's kind of—"

"Never mind, I know." Sara shrugged. "It's complicated."

"No nests yet," Izzy announced one Friday afternoon a couple of weeks later as we wandered Turtle Beach. She dropped onto the hot white sand and leaned back on her elbows.

"It's too soon," I said. "You tired?"

"No, just lazy."

She'd been missing more school lately, a day here, a day there. The radiation was over for the time being, but she was still worn out after a full day of school. She looked so frail. I understood why Rosa spent her days pouring fatty concoctions down Izzy. The delicate bones of her face were too evident, and her eyes had a lost, childlike look.

I sat down next to Izzy and we watched an elaborate sandcastle, obviously the work of many hours, melt into the water, dissolving like sugar as the waves licked at it.

"I did it, finally. I told Sam I loved him," Izzy announced brightly. "To which he responded that he was afraid he was falling for me. I take that to be as good as the basic *I love you.* Although I would have preferred better phrasing."

I stared at the sand. "I'm really happy for you, Iz," I managed at last.

"You'll find a guy just as great, you know."

"I know."

"Even my parents love him," Izzy said. "Sometimes I think it's too good to be true. I'm not hallucinating, am I? I mean, some of those drugs I'm taking are pretty potent."

"If you are hallucinating, would you mind conjuring up a cute guy for me?"

Izzy laughed. We fell silent, watching the timid waves. The water was quiet that day, and so was the beach. Thick gray clouds banked on the horizon, and the air was flat and humid. I realized that this was the first time we'd been back to this spot since the day Izzy had told me she was sick.

"When I die, I want my ashes scattered here," Izzy said suddenly.

I froze. Not *if* I die. *When.*

"Not by the water; everyone does that," she continued. "In the grass over here, where we found the nest."

I kept my gaze on the sandcastle, now a smooth, brown, shapeless mass, like a modern sculpture. "I don't know if I want to be cremated," I said, just a casual response to a casual conversation. "I don't like the box-in-the-ground thing. I'm too claustrophobic. But I keep thinking the burning would hurt. Which is crazy, of course." I was babbling, but I couldn't stop. "I kind of like the water burial idea—canoe out to sea, play a nice sea chantey or something. I read once that in the Solomon Islands, they just lay you on a reef to be eaten by sharks."

"Nice," Izzy said. "Ashes to ashes, dust to shark. All part of the great cosmic continuum. The scientist in me likes that." She rolled on her side, watching me. "What do you think happens when you die, Al?"

"I don't know," I said softly. "I'd like to think you go to a place without zits and static cling. But I can't find a religion that buys into that notion."

"Rosa's does. She's into a full-service heaven. She goes to church, like, three times a week to pray for me, did I tell you? It's sort of unnerving. I told her thanks, but still, I'd rather have her embroider me another sweater. It seems more practical under the circumstances."

She was telling me she knew. She'd known all along, but I wouldn't admit it to myself and neither

137

would Lauren and Miguel and, probably, Sam. We were cowards, all of us. Izzy had let us off the hook, making it easy for us to pretend everything was fine.

Only now, at last, she was getting tired of the pretending.

I could feel my insides twisting, my eyes getting ready to churn out tears. This was my chance to help her through this, and I couldn't.

It wasn't my place, I told myself; she should be talking to her mom and dad. But I was her best friend. Best friends were created so you could say all the things you could never say to parents. Things like *I know I'm dying, and I'm afraid.*

But there was nothing I could say that would make her feel better, no easy lie, nothing. That's what I was good at, little white lies that made people happy. I would have told her what she wanted to hear, but this time I didn't know what it was.

"Remember that day we came here?" I said, watching the waves creep up, then retreat. "Why didn't you tell me sooner about being sick, Iz?"

"What difference would it have made, in the grand scheme of things?"

"You weren't honest with me, though."

"Are you mad?"

"I was," I said. The waves gulped down the last of the castle. "But then I realized you'd done it because you wanted to protect me."

Izzy cleared her throat. "Al, my mom's starting

to talk about going to Miami, getting an apartment there."

"But why?"

For the first time I thought Izzy might lose it. She was shuddering and hugging her knees, and her mouth was quivering with the effort to keep from crying. She looked like one of those old china figurines with all the little cracks beneath the surface, the kind my grandmother collected. I knew if she started to cry, she'd crumble into the sand in a million pieces and I'd never put her back together.

"Tell me, Iz," I soothed. "It'll be okay."

"She says she thinks I'll get better care there if anything comes up. But I don't want to go back there, Al. It's like a waiting room for the dying." She started to sob, a sweet, childish sob, as if she didn't have the energy for any more than that.

I put my arms around her. I didn't know what to say. There was this big, horrible hole where the words were supposed to go.

"Wherever you go, I'll come be with you," I promised.

"You can't do that," she sobbed. "It won't be that way. There'll be school and stuff."

She closed her eyes, and I could see her make a conscious effort to compose herself. "Who knows?" she asked quietly. "Maybe I'll just die in my sleep, in my own bed. That would be the way to go."

She wiped her eyes and pulled away, embarrassed, and struggled to her feet. "I'm really sorry," she said. "Just a little exercise in self-pity. The pain medicine makes me weepy."

"Don't be sorry. Don't be." I stood too. I fumbled with my backpack, digging out my keys, stalling for time.

I was failing her. I was pretending because pretending was easier.

I made myself meet her frightened eyes. Maybe it was better to be honest and do it badly than to lie and do it well.

"You know what I think, Iz?"

She sniffled. "What?"

"I think," I said slowly, finding my way to the words, "that when people die, it's sort of like . . . well, like the turtles."

I was afraid she might laugh at me, but she didn't.

"What I mean is, we have a responsibility to keep them around so other generations can see them. To make sure they survive. I think it's the same way with people. It's our job to keep a part of the people we care about around. Even, you know, after they're gone."

I stared at the spot where the castle had been. It was just wet brown sand, flat and featureless. "I don't know what happens when you die, Iz. But I do know that if I ever lose you, you'll always be with me. Forever." I fell silent for a moment. "I'm sorry. I don't know what to say. Or maybe I just don't know how to say it."

Izzy followed my gaze to the sand and the endless water beyond it. "Yes," she said, very softly. "Yes, you do."

Chapter Twelve

THE NEXT MORNING the sound of the phone cut through my murky dreams. Rain clattered against the window like impatient, tapping fingers.

I waited for Sara to get the phone; it was Saturday, after all. Then I remembered. My parents had dropped her off at the site of the basketball tournament for an early practice, then headed on to the clinic, which was open till two on Saturday.

I grabbed the receiver. "Yeah?" I said, half buried under my quilt.

"Alison, it's Sam."

I jerked up, instantly awake. "What? Is Izzy okay?"

"No, no, it's not Iz. It's Morgan." I heard the whir of an electric drill. "I'm at the garage, see, and I would have called Izzy, but she was really beat last night. . . ."

"Is there a problem with Morgan?"

A sigh. "Not unless you consider being arrested a problem. They found him on Clementine again. Jane went over to check on him and when she saw that he and the horse were gone, she called me. I was trying to get off work when the cops called to say they had this old guy over at the station who claimed he knew me." He gave a short laugh. "Some poor cop had to drag that horse down Route 41 in the rain. They weren't amused."

"I'll go bail him out," I said. "Don't worry."

"Jane would have gone, but she lent her daughter the car. I hate to ask, but the thing is, my boss says that if I split one more time, I'm out of a job."

"It's okay, Sam. Really. I don't mind. I like Morgan."

"He promised me," Sam said. "I really thought I'd gotten through to him, you know?"

"It'll be okay," I said, even though I didn't think it would.

"Could you just pick him up? There's no fine or anything, I don't think, but if there is, you know I'll pay you back."

I'd never heard such uncertainty in his voice before, and it made me sad.

"I'll take him back to the trailer and stay with him till you get off work. Take your time. We'll play some poker."

I heard metallic pounding, a muffled curse, more whirring. "Crap. Oh, crap."

"What, Sam?"

"The damn horse."

"I'll figure something out. You'd better get back to work."

"I owe you. I'll be home as soon as I can."

"Don't worry, Sam. It'll all work out."

I hung up the phone and sneered at my reflection in the dresser mirror. "Liar," I said.

I threw on my rain slicker and riding boots, grabbed a granola bar for me, and sliced an apple for Clementine. I found the car keys after a ten-minute search through the living room, then ran out to the barn to hay and water Snickers. To my surprise, it was already done, the stall even mucked out. Sara? I grabbed a rope and ran to the car. It gurgled and coughed before settling into an uneasy idle. Rain sheeted the windows. This was not, I decided, a promising start to the day.

Clementine was tethered to a tree by the side of the police station. I parked the car and went over to reassure her with a couple of apple slices. She looked bewildered but content, very much like Morgan looked when I located him in the station, sitting placidly on a bench.

"Morgan," I said, kneeling in front of him. "Do you remember me? Alison?"

His eyes were cloudy. "I'm going to Wisconsin," he said.

"How about we go home instead? What about

Cha–cha and the dogs? You can't go to Wisconsin without them."

"You ever play keno?"

"No, but maybe later we could play a hand of poker."

"I have to take a piss."

I pushed back my slicker hood. I very much wished I'd had a cup of coffee before leaving.

"There's the can over there," a jowly policeman told me. "Then we can take care of the paperwork. You the relative?"

"I'm the friend of the relative."

"Nice old guy, but he oughta be . . . you know."

I took Morgan's hand. It was as light and fragile as a little kite.

He followed me obediently to the door of the men's room. "This is the bathroom," I said.

He looked at me, profoundly surprised.

"You said . . . you know. You wanted to . . . be here."

He reached for the handle, poised to act, then stopped, suspended, as if his batteries had run out.

"I have to piss," he said.

"Stay here."

I went back to the policeman. He was typing, two-fingered, on a computer keyboard. "How old is that nag, anyway?" he asked me. "About a hundred?"

"Pretty old. You didn't find any stray dogs or parrots when you picked Morgan up, did you?"

"Nope. You want to file a missing parrot report?" He did not smile.

"No, that won't be necessary. But I have a problem. Morgan needs to use the rest room."

"How exactly is that your problem?"

"I think he's . . . uh, having second thoughts."

The cop looked over his shoulder. He rubbed his thick jaw.

"These old farts, I know it's hard, but you gotta put them somewhere for their own good, kid."

"Maybe you're right. Could you, uh . . . give him some moral support?"

"I'm not good with old people." He went back to his typing. "Too bad," he added under his breath. "I'm stuck here in the land of the living dead."

I went back to the rest room. Morgan still stood there, paralyzed by indecision.

I opened the door a crack. "Anyone in there?"

My voice echoed off the yellow-tiled walls. No one answered.

I took Morgan's hand and led him into the bathroom. I'd never seen a urinal before. I was not impressed.

I stood him before the first one. "I'll wait for you outside," I promised. "Don't worry."

"I have to piss," he said.

"Then you've come to the right place."

I slipped outside and waited, feeling frustrated and weary. I wondered how Sam could stand the relentless strain of caring for his grandfather.

After a long time Morgan emerged. He smiled at me without the slightest glimmer of recognition. "I'm going to Vegas," he said.

"Come on," I said. "I'll drive."

I talked one of the cops into driving Morgan home, pointing out that otherwise they were going to be stuck with a very wet, very old horse. I left my car there and rode Clementine back to the trailer. It wasn't far, but we were both soaked to the bone by the time we got there.

Jane was waiting in the trailer, and she tended to Morgan while I got Clementine warm and settled.

"Girl, let's get some hot tea in you," Jane said when I stepped inside, making little puddles wherever I stood.

I shook off my slicker. "Caffeine sounds like a fine idea."

"Darn, I wish I had my car," Jane said. "But my daughter wrecked hers again and I lent her my Toyota for the week. Otherwise I could take you back to the station and you could be on your way."

While the water rumbled in the kettle and the rain drummed down on the trailer, we started a game of poker, at Morgan's suggestion. He fell asleep before the kettle whistled. I covered him with his old quilt, and the dogs huddled around him, a motley, breathing quilt of their own design.

"What's happening?" Cha-cha asked.

"Shh, Morgan's sleeping," Jane said.

"It's nice of you to help Sam out the way you have," I whispered as Jane and I huddled near the tiny, ancient stove.

"I don't mind. My husband had Alzheimer's, and I know what it's like. I admire the kid for trying." When she smiled, all the lines in her strong, proud face rearranged themselves, like a shifting kaleidoscope. "I just think he's got to wise up. He's killing himself working, and he's got the problems at school and all."

I sipped the tea, warming my numb fingers on the chipped teacup. "Problems?"

"If I'd known they were going to suspend Sam, I would have stepped in, maybe taken Morgan in during the day. Thing is, I work part-time filling in as cashier at the Mobil on Route 301, and—"

"They suspended Sam?"

"He didn't tell you? Great, Jane, and now you've gone and talked your mouth off. Well, it's a cinch you would've figured it out soon enough."

We heard the low growl of Sam's motorcycle and the crunch of gravel. He stepped into the trailer, bringing the smell of rain with him. His face was flushed.

He went straight over to check Morgan, who didn't awaken.

"Man, I'm sorry," Sam said to us. "Jack wouldn't let me off till now. I tried, but . . . He's okay?"

"He's fine," I said. "I think he enjoyed himself."

"What happened at the police station?"

"Morgan went to the bathroom. That was pretty much the high point."

"No ticket, nothing like that?"

"No. They see this a lot, I think."

He frowned. "He's been doing really well, hasn't he, Jane? Staying in, watching TV. He really seemed to understand." He slumped against the wall. "I ought to get rid of that damn horse, that's the problem here."

"Sam." Jane ran her hand over his wet hair affectionately. "That horse isn't the problem."

"Where is Clementine, anyway?" Sam asked me.

"I rode her home," I said. "She's all set."

"No wonder you're soaked." He paced back and forth, not an easy task in the tiny space available. "So your car's still back at the station?"

I nodded, sipping my tea. His agitation filled the trailer, making it feel as if Sam, not the rain and wind, were the cause of its vibrating and shuddering.

"I can give you a lift back on the bike," Sam said.

"Wait till the rain slows," Jane said. "You shouldn't ride that contraption in this weather, Sam."

I shrugged. "It doesn't matter. I'm already soaked."

"I've got to pick up some groceries on the way back," Sam said to Jane. "What can I get you?"

Jane frowned. "You are one stubborn young

149

man. A quart of milk, then, if you insist on going. Low-fat, not skim, okay? I'll stay here with the Lone Ranger till you get back."

"Thanks, Jane." Sam gave her a quick, shy kiss on the cheek, and she smiled with pleasure.

We rode through the rain in silence. By the time we reached the police station I was shivering, even though it was warm and muggy. I climbed off the bike and handed Sam my helmet.

"Have you got a minute?" I asked.

"I owe you a lot more than that."

I motioned to my car and he followed.

We climbed in. It was a relief to be out of the rain, even though we were soaked. I turned on the car and cranked the heater. "Why didn't you tell us about school?" I asked. "Izzy or me?"

Sam shrugged. "It just happened the day before yesterday. And anyway, I didn't want to hear a lot of second-guessing. I've heard just about all of that I can take."

"Oh?"

"They called my mom in Michigan and told her what was going on, not that she didn't already know. So she calls me and tells me she really thinks it's time for me to give up this whole notion, that it would be better for Morgan and for me if we went ahead and put him in a home, as much as she hates to do it."

"What did you say?"

"I said, 'You didn't exactly give up on Dad overnight, did you? You hung in there.' To which she said she'd hung in way too long." He pounded the dashboard. "Sorry. I'm just pissed off at all these people telling me what's best for me. This is about what's best for Morgan."

"You're right. I'm sure you can figure something out," I said automatically.

"Thanks." He reached across and touched my shoulder. "It's nice to have someone on my side."

"What does Izzy say about all this?"

"We don't talk about it much. She's been so worn out lately, I hate to bother her with it."

A policeman, the heavyset one I'd talked to at the station, crossed the lot to his car. I thought of my morning with Morgan. Of the blank, content, confused stare, and the hand as vulnerable as a baby bird.

"Sam," I said suddenly, before I lost my nerve, "this is wrong. I was wrong before. You can't work it out. You've got to realize the truth. Morgan needs more care than you can give him. Can't you see? You're hurting yourself and you're going to end up hurting him. Your mom's right, Sam. Morgan needs someone to be there for him all the time."

He gazed at me with such wounded eyes that I wanted to take it all back. I touched his arm and he recoiled. "You tried better than anyone else could have. You are good at watching out for people, Sam, you're the best. But things change. You can't stop Morgan from getting old. You do what you can do, but some things you can't change."

Suddenly I realized that if he put Morgan in a nursing home, he would have no reason to stay in Florida—no reason except Izzy, and maybe me. I would lose him forever. But then, I reminded myself, I'd probably already lost him.

"I'm sorry," I said. "I was just trying to be honest."

"What the hell do you know about honesty?"

"Not a whole lot," I admitted. The rain was pelting down with more force. "Look. Rosa works at a nursing home; maybe I could talk to her. Or your mom could give her a call, maybe set something up."

"You don't know a damn thing about loyalty, do you, Alison? When you love someone, you don't change your mind halfway down the road. You don't decide, whoops, would you mind dating my best friend instead of me? And you don't say, hey, you're getting in the way, so I'm going to lock you up in some warehouse for the dying."

He leapt out, slamming the door behind him. I couldn't tell if he was crying or if it was just the rain. I thought about all the lies I could say to make him feel okay. I thought of how much it hurt to see someone you loved in such pain. And then I drove away.

My mom was in the kitchen when I got home, still in her white vet coat. "You're home already?" she asked.

I tossed my slicker aside. "What do you mean, already?" I asked shakily. "Where's Dad?"

"He had an emergency. Never mind where's Dad, where's Sara?"

I slapped my forehead. "Oh, great, just great. Oh, jeez, she's going to kill me."

"You forgot?"

"I had an emergency of my own. Sam's grandfather was at the police station—long story." I grabbed her wrist to check the time. "Do you think it's too late?"

"It should just be finishing up by now. Damn. I was counting on you, Alison, since your father and I couldn't be there, and it was so important to her."

"I'll make it up to her."

"Please try. I think she's feeling a little neglected."

I started to leave, but my mom took my arm. "Honey. I have to tell you something."

Her somber gaze was all I needed. My heart dropped. "Oh, God, is it Izzy?"

She nodded. "Lauren called me at work when she couldn't get you. She didn't want to leave a message on the machine. Izzy had another seizure this morning, a bad one, and they're taking her back to Miami for tests."

"When?"

"Right away. They arranged for one of those transport ambulances." She took my shoulders and held them firmly. "She's okay. It's just a setback, not . . ."

"She doesn't want to be there. She told me so."

"Lauren likes the doctors there. They know Izzy's case, they can do what's best for her."

"I have to go see her."

"Maybe we can work something out next week. I could take the day off, rearrange some appointments, and we could go together."

"No, Mom, I have to see her right away. Let me take the wagon, okay?"

"Alison, don't put me in this position." She leaned against the kitchen counter. Her eyes were damp. Thunder rolled, rattling the windowpanes. "The weather's terrible, and you know that car's been acting up. I can't let you go, so don't ask."

"I drive it around town."

"Just for quick errands. This is a long trip. Hon, why is it so important? A few days won't matter."

"Because I promised. Because it could matter."

"I'm really sorry, Alison. But the answer is no."

I bit my lower lip to stop the quivering. "Did Lauren call Sam?" I asked at last.

"She said she tried, but there was no answer at the trailer."

I looked up Sam's number and dialed it. Jane answered. "Is Sam back yet?" I asked.

"Not yet," she said. "You want to leave a message?"

"Yes. No, I'll call back," I said, and hung up. "I'm going to change my clothes and go get Sara," I said.

My mom nodded. She was crying softly, and I realized she wasn't handling this any better than I was. I went to her and we hugged for a while. I felt better, even though I knew she couldn't fix anything, and I couldn't either.

Chapter Thirteen

SARA WAS WAITING by the gym, her basketball tucked under her arm, her face hardened into a scowl. In her right hand she held a little silver trophy.

She slammed the door so hard I jumped. "We won, not that you give a—"

"Sara, you have to understand. I wanted to be here, but something came up."

She stared at her trophy. "Look, I'm not a moron. I know you *think* I'm a moron, but eventually even I get the picture. You don't want to have anything to do with me, fine."

"It was about Morgan. He went riding Clementine again, only this time he got busted. I had to bail him out of jail because Sam couldn't get away."

For the first time, she looked at me. "Is he all right?"

"Well, yes and no."

"Did they lock him up and everything?"

"No. Nothing that dramatic. I wish you'd been there, though. I could have used some help. I had to take him to the bathroom. The guys' bathroom. It's been a very full morning."

She conceded a small smile, nothing more.

"Can I see your trophy?" I asked.

Grudgingly she handed it to me. It was plastic painted silver, a crude likeness of a girl leaping up with a basketball on the tip of her finger.

"It's stupid, I know," Sara said.

"I've never won a trophy," I pointed out.

I returned it to her. She had chipped pink polish on her stubby fingernails. "When did you start wearing nail polish?" I asked.

"I don't know. A while ago. Kayla had some."

"I've been sort of preoccupied lately, haven't I?"

Sara gave a terse nod. Tears filled her eyes.

"I guess I've been worried about Izzy and Sam and everything."

"That's not why," Sara muttered. "It started before that. It started—I don't know, a real long time ago. When you got to high school."

"What started?"

"You . . . I don't know, Al, you just . . . changed. I feel like—" She swallowed. "I feel like I can't keep up."

"You're not supposed to keep up." I played with her ponytail gently. "You're ten, you're supposed to be ten. When you're growing up, there are all these stages, some of which, incidentally, pretty much suck. But you can't leave any out."

"Why not?"

"Because . . . It's hard to explain. It's like when you play Monopoly. If you skipped any of the spaces, it would be cheating."

"I feel like you live on a different planet from me sometimes," Sara said.

I laughed. "Sometimes so do I."

"I'm not a total moron, you know. You can tell me stuff."

"I know I can," I said. "I'm sorry if I forgot that for a while."

Suddenly I thought of Izzy, far away in an ambulance, slicing through the rain to a place she didn't want to be. "Sara, Izzy's sicker," I said softly. "They're taking her to that hospital in Miami."

"Is she going to—"

"I don't know."

She nodded. "It's okay about the game," she said after a while. "Sometimes . . . you know. Things get complicated."

We were halfway home when the car began to shudder as if it had a raging fever. It coughed, it sighed, and then it gave out. I managed to ease off onto the shoulder before we lost momentum.

I looked at Sara and smiled wearily. "It would, of course, be raining."

"There's a gas station about a mile down the road."

"Do you believe a day can be cursed?"

"It'll be okay, Al. Want me to go call, and you stay here?"

I put on the flashers. "No. We'll go together."

The rain was colder now, harder too. We sloshed along, side by side, getting drenched by passing cars. Sam's place wasn't far. We could have walked there and used the phone, but I just couldn't deal with him yet, not face to face. When I got home, when I was dry and calm, then I would call and tell him about Izzy.

Sara noticed the motorcycle before I did. It whizzed past, then made a U-turn, circled back, and came to a stop behind us.

Sam, of course. He was carrying a plastic grocery bag, the top tied in a knot to keep out the rain.

"I guess it's my turn to rescue you," he said flatly. He was still angry. "Come on, I'll take you to the trailer. You can call your parents or whatever from there. Sara, you first." He cast me a guarded look. "I'll be right back."

I kept on walking, and in a few minutes he was back for me. I climbed on the back of the bike and reached for his waist. I was surprised when I began to cry, because it was the last thing I wanted to do. "Izzy's worse," I said, my cheek against his wet, slick jacket. "They took her to Miami."

Sam gave a brief nod. We rode in silence back to

the trailer. With Morgan and Jane and Sara there, not to mention all the animals, it was impossible to move. The air was stale and damp.

Sam threw his jacket in a corner. "When did Izzy go?"

"This morning. Lauren tried to call you. I was going to, when I got home."

I sat down between the two poodles on the edge of Morgan's bed. I could not look at Sam. "I'm afraid she's going to die," I whispered. "I have to go see her."

Sam ran his fingers through his wet hair. "I'll take the bike."

I looked at him hopefully.

"I can't take you," he said, "it's not safe. The damn weather—"

"Oh, but it's okay for you to go?" Jane demanded. "No sir, mister, you are doing no such thing."

He rolled his eyes at her, his anger softened by affection. "Who elected you mom?"

"You need a mom while you're here," she said gruffly.

"I wanted to take the wagon," I said, watching absently as Cha-cha climbed onto Sara's shoulder. "But my mom said it wasn't reliable. I guess she had a point."

"Give me five," Cha-cha said.

Morgan, who was sitting on the couch, began shuffling cards. "Five-card stud?" he suggested to Sara.

"I could take the bus," I said.

"What's the hurry, sweetie? Is she that sick?" Jane asked gently.

I nodded. My throat was tight and my hands were trembling. I couldn't tell them that I knew Izzy would be gone soon. I didn't know how I knew. Something remote in her eyes that day at the beach, maybe. Even then, I could see she was leaving us.

"You know, they might not even let you in," Jane said. "You know how hospitals are."

"She doesn't want to be there, Sam," I said.

"I know." He was clenching and unclenching his fists. "I know."

"Aces high," Morgan said.

"Nice caboose," Cha-cha told Sara.

"Thank you," she said politely, her eyes on me. Morgan got up. He shuffled to the little bathroom that was separated from the main room by an accordion partition.

"If I had my car," Jane said, "goodness knows I'd lend it to you kids." She shook her head. "Maybe it's just as well. Things like that aren't pretty. Maybe it's better you think of her like she used to be."

"No," I said, sobbing softly. "I promised her. She can't be there all by herself. She wanted to be here, she wanted to die in her own bed. . . ."

Sam grabbed his jacket. "I'm going outside," he said. "I need some air."

Jane sighed softly. "Tea," she said. "I'll make us all some tea."

Morgan emerged. He rocked toward me like one of those wobbly windup toys, then stopped and took my hand in his. "What?" I asked, and then I knew.

In my hand was a set of keys.

"Are these to the Cadillac?" I whispered.

He nodded. I searched his eyes. He looked vaguely pleased with himself. "You're lending me the Cadillac?"

"That car's a hundred years old!" Jane exclaimed.

"I want to go," Sara said.

I stared at the keys doubtfully. Morgan shuffled away. He retrieved his sweater and his leather driving cap.

"Morgan," I said. "This wouldn't be Vegas, this wouldn't be Wisconsin."

"Hop in, hop in," Morgan said, inching toward the door. "We haven't got all day."

Sara tugged on my arm. "Can I come?"

"Sara, that'll just complicate—" I saw her downcast eyes and caught myself. "You know what?" I said. "I think I'd like that. I could really use the moral support."

"You do realize Mom'll kill us, don't you?" she said gleefully.

"I'll call her and tell her," I said. "Let's just hope I get the answering machine."

"No, let me," Sara said. "I can handle her."

I hesitated. "Okay, then. Sure."

Morgan signaled the dogs and they arranged themselves in a perfect line at the door, waiting patiently, it didn't matter for what. Cha-cha flew to his shoulder.

Sara dialed our number and gave me a thumbs-up. "Machine," she whispered.

"Nice caboose," Cha-cha told Jane.

She rolled her eyes. "Hush, you nasty bird."

"Hello, Mom?" Sara said. "Darn, I hoped you'd be there. It's Sara. Al and me and Sam's grandpa and four dogs and a parrot are going to see Izzy. We have a car, I think maybe it's an antique. We'll be back, um . . ." She looked to me.

I threw up my hands.

"In a jiffy," Jane offered.

"In a Jeffy," Sara said. "Oh, yeah, we won the tournament. We totally slaughtered them. Bye." She hung up. "Well?"

"Excellent," I said.

"What's happening?" Cha-cha asked.

Jane put her arm around Morgan's shoulders. "Sweetie, why don't you stay here with me and keep me company? You don't want to go on a long car trip. They can be so boring."

Morgan stared at her blankly. "It'll do forty-five," he said.

"I know, sweetie. Come, come. Take off your sweater. You let the kids go on and do what they have to."

Morgan let himself be led to a chair. I leaned

163

down and kissed him on the cheek. "Thank you, Morgan," I whispered. "You too, Jane."

I opened the door. The rain had slowed. The sky looked angry and bruised. Sam was standing near his bike. Sara ran past me to the Cadillac, dancing in the rain, thrilled to be going on such an adventure, forgetting what our destination was. That was okay, I thought. She was still just a kid. And I was glad she was coming with me.

I turned. Morgan was watching me with those untroubled, accepting eyes. "It'll do forty-five," he said.

"We're not going to Vegas, Morgan," I said gently.

He adjusted his driving cap. "One last ride."

I looked over at Jane. She was shaking her head.

"Oh, what the hell," I said. "Come on, Morgan." I took his hand, his featherlight hand. "Let's hit the road and see where it goes."

He stood, and for a moment I thought I saw something more in his eyes, sun behind clouds. Or maybe I just wanted to. "After this, Vegas," he said. "Have you ever played keno?"

We walked to the car. The animals followed. I opened the back door, and Morgan and the dogs and Cha-cha climbed in. Sara joined them on the other side.

Sam ran over as I settled in the front seat. "What the hell are you doing?"

I rolled the window down. "We're going to see Izzy," I said, trying to locate the ignition.

"After that, who knows? Maybe Vegas."

"You can't drive this thing, it's a dinosaur." He ran to Morgan's door and opened it. "And where did you get those keys? I hid those keys in my locker. What the hell is going on, Morgan? You had an extra set? You were holding out on me, your own grandson?"

Morgan smiled, pure and blank as a newborn.

The rain picked up again, pelting down with renewed force. I managed to find the clutch. "This is just like a normal car, right?"

Sam returned to my window. "Why are you doing this?"

"I have to, Sam. You do what you have to do."

Sam glared at me. "You are one very interesting girl, Alison." He said it without a trace of a smile.

I cranked the ignition. Sam opened the door. He gazed at me, at Sara, at Morgan and the menagerie.

"Move over," he said at last. "I'll drive."

"Why you? That's kind of sexist."

"Because I'll get us there faster. Isn't that the whole idea?"

I considered, then slid across the wide bench seat. Sam climbed in. His face was wet. He clutched the wheel. In the back, the dogs panted rhythmically. The rain made a snapping sound on the fabric roof.

"Hit the road," Morgan instructed.

"In a minute." Sam turned to me. The anger had gentled. "What are you going to say to Izzy?"

he asked me, in a voice so restrained I could barely hear him.

"I don't know. Maybe I'll tell her the truth."

Sam stole a glance at Morgan. "The truth, like you told it to me today?"

"Isn't that what you wanted me to do with Izzy?"

Sam closed his eyes. "Yes. I don't know. Maybe, but not now, not when she's so sick."

"That's what I thought, too. But the other day, on the beach, Izzy was talking about dying. And I started to think maybe I was being selfish, not being completely honest with her. Protecting myself, not her."

"Maybe the truth about how all this started doesn't matter now," Sam said. "Maybe all that matters is that I care for Izzy now, and so do you."

"Maybe. I just don't know anymore."

Sam looked over at me, and I wanted to say, "I miss you, please don't be angry with me, let's not go on this awful trip as enemies." But silence stretched between us.

"Hit the road," Morgan said again.

Sam cranked the car, the poodles barked, and then we were off, at a breathtaking forty-five miles per hour.

Five hours thirty-five minutes and nine rest stops later (five at Morgan's request, three by Sara and Sam and me, and one by the dogs), we arrived

166

in Miami. It was dark by the time we found the hospital, and visiting hours were almost over.

"I want to see Izzy too," Sara said as Sam eased the big Cadillac into a parking space.

"Sara, I don't know if that's a good idea," Sam said. "She's really sick, kid."

"No," I said. "Let her come. She can handle it."

"What about Morgan, then?" Sam asked. "I guess we could go up in shifts."

"Let's all go," I said. "We won't be long. We'll crack the windows and the dogs will be fine."

"I don't know about this," Sam said.

"Trust me," I said. "Izzy will be glad."

We located Lauren and Miguel and talked to them for a few minutes before the four of us headed to Izzy's room. A crisp-looking nurse at the main desk asked Sara how old she was.

"Thirteen," she said coolly, without missing a beat.

The nurse nodded and let us through.

It was dark in Izzy's room. A little bedside lamp provided a thin white tube of light. Izzy was asleep. An IV tube snaked out of her arm. Her head was uncovered and she had on the red pajamas I'd given her.

We stood at the foot of her bed, all of us. I didn't know whether to wake her or not. And even if I did, I didn't know what I would say.

I went to her side. Her hand was smooth, light, weightless as Morgan's. She opened her eyes.

"Hey," she whispered. "Look who's here. And me with my hair a mess."

"I told you I would."

"How'd you get here?" Her voice was slurred, like a sound underwater.

"Morgan's Cadillac. There are four dogs and a parrot dying to come up and say hi. Sam's here, too. And Sara and Morgan."

She laughed softly. "Come here, guys."

Sara took Morgan's hand and they went to the other side of her bed.

"We won our basketball tournament, Iz," Sara said shyly. "We slaughtered them completely. I won a trophy. I wish I'd brought it; I would have given it to you."

"That's okay. You hang on to it. You know I can't dribble to save my life."

Sara bit her lip. "Does it hurt?" she whispered.

"Not much. I promise." Izzy turned to Morgan. "Morgan, you been getting into trouble?"

Morgan stared at her doubtfully.

"That's okay, guy," Izzy said. "This place freaks me out too. Sara, maybe you should take Morgan out in the hall for a second, okay?"

Sara nodded. She tugged on Morgan's arm, but he refused to move. His mouth worked, but he didn't speak.

"Come on, Morgan," Sara said.

Suddenly Morgan reached for Izzy's hand. He bent down slowly and brought it to his lips, then met Izzy's gaze. A smile passed between them.

"See ya, Morgan," Izzy whispered.

Morgan let himself be led away, and Izzy turned to me. Her eyes were filled with tears.

"God, this death stuff sucks," she said. "I'm not even going to see the damn turtles, Al."

"Of course you'll see the damn turtles."

"No, I won't." She squeezed my hand weakly. "Don't lie to me, okay? Not anymore. I'm so doped up you could tell me anything and I'd believe you."

I looked at Sam. He was standing at the end of the bed, clutching the metal railing. "Okay, Iz," he said.

There, I thought, *there it is. We can tell her the truth.*

"I never even got to be a lousy guinea pig," Izzy said. "So much for changing the world."

"Izzy," I said, "you changed *my* world."

A tear rolled down her cheek. "There's that, I guess," she said. "That's something."

"That's everything," I whispered, and then I realized my own tears were falling all over her arm, her blanket, everywhere.

Izzy closed her eyes and fell silent. For a moment I thought she'd passed out. Then, with effort, she opened them again.

"Just promise me one thing," she said, her voice barely audible.

"Name it," I sobbed.

"The twins in Paris. Don't forget."

"I won't."

"Scratch that. It doesn't have to be twins. Just

get yourself to Paris. With the right guy." She gave a slight smile. "Me, I could have handled the twins."

She looked over at Sam and I stepped back, searching in vain for some Kleenex. I found some by the next bed, an empty one behind a half-drawn curtain. When I came back, Sam was clutching Izzy's hand. Tears rolled freely down his face.

I paused by the curtain, knowing I still had more to say. For once, just once, I wanted to say the right thing. Not what I thought she wanted to hear. Just what was right. But it was Sam's turn now. I would wait, then I would tell her, then, maybe, we would go.

Sam leaned over Izzy without saying a word. Their lips met, gently, tenderly, her hand on his shoulder, and they kissed forever. When they parted he whispered something to her.

I couldn't hear the words, but I could see her eyes and I could see his lips.

And I knew from Izzy's radiant smile that hearing Sam say "I love you" meant more than any truth I might have found to tell her. I knew that he did love her, even as much, perhaps, as I did. And I was glad.

Chapter Fourteen

"THANK YOU."

Sam took a long drag on his cigarette. "For what?" he asked.

We were sitting on a bench near the entrance to the hospital. Bugs swirled in the circle of fluorescent light over our heads. "For that. For the way you said good-bye. For . . . I don't know, for loving Izzy."

He gave me a dubious look. "I don't get it, Alison. You're so damn accepting about all this. Look at the mess we've created."

"What mess?"

"Well, for starters—" He took another long, slow drag. "For starters, I'm in love with you and your best friend, who happens to be up in that stinking hospital room dying. And your sister and my grandfather, who thinks he's going to Wisconsin

171

to press cheese or else Vegas to play blackjack, are down in the cafeteria, where he's teaching her to cheat at poker. And in a Cadillac in the parking lot, four dogs and a parrot are crapping all over the back-seat. For starters."

"Sara already knows how to play poker," I pointed out.

Sam tossed his cigarette and we watched it glow hot, then die. He lit another one methodically, making a point of it.

"You're smoking again," I said.

He inhaled deeply, ignoring me.

"How come you're so good at taking care of Morgan and so lousy at taking care of yourself?" I demanded. "You're suspended from school, you're about to lose your job, you're smoking, and, frankly, while we're on the subject, you need a haircut."

He managed a sardonic half-smile.

"Okay, so that's a judgment call," I said. "My point is, you're lousing up your life trying to do something impossible. You can't make Morgan not get old, Sam. There are some things we just can't change. How can you stand there by Izzy's bed and not realize that? There are cycles to life. Izzy knows that. And I think Morgan knows that. Even if you don't."

He looked at me sharply. "What makes you say that about Morgan?"

I sighed. Suddenly I felt very tired. "It's hard to explain. Before we got in the car to leave today, he said to me, 'One last ride,' like he knew things were going to change soon."

"He also said he was going to put two grand down on thirty-two red when we got to Vegas. He doesn't know what he's saying half the time. He doesn't even know who he is half the time."

I touched Sam's knee. "Then it doesn't matter, does it? All of this really matters only to you."

Sam took one last puff on the cigarette, stared at it, then tossed it aside. "We should go," he said.

I didn't move. "When I first got to know you, Sam, I wondered if maybe you didn't care that much about your life."

"Yeah, the death wish theory," he said flatly.

"Laugh if you want. But when we first met, you were lying in a ditch, wrapped around your bike, soon to be bleeding all over my best T-shirt."

"You said it was old."

"I lied." I paused. "I just don't understand how you can treat yourself so badly and then be so good with Morgan."

Sam stared past me. "Because I owe him."

"But someone has to take care of you, Sam. I know your parents weren't all that hot at it when you were growing up. But that doesn't mean you have to continue the tradition." My voice was rising. "I mean, Izzy's lying up there dying, and she doesn't have a damn choice. But you do. We do."

We sat there for a while, listening to the bugs click against the light. I checked my watch. I needed to call my mom and gather up Sara and Morgan. We still had a long drive ahead of us, and Sam and I weren't getting anywhere.

I stood. "You're right. I guess we should get going."

Sam stared at the ground. "I know it sounds crazy, Alison. But I'd really miss him. I liked being responsible for him. Even if I blew it."

"You didn't blow it. You did the best you could. You made him happy for a while longer. The same with Izzy, too. Those are good things, even if they didn't end up all neat and happy and tied up with a little bow."

"Come on." Sam stood abruptly, sighing. "We've got a long trip home."

"I'm glad we came."

"Yeah, I am too." He paused. "What happens now, I wonder?"

"We hit the road, I guess."

Sam nodded grimly. "And see where it goes."

Four days later Izzy slipped into a coma. A week and a half after that, she died. They had a traditional service at a church, but afterward we all went down to the beach and Lauren and Miguel scattered her ashes there.

They hadn't wanted to. Sam and I had had to convince them that was what Izzy had wanted. In the end they relented, and I was glad we could do something for Izzy even when she was gone. Rosa said it was sacrilegious, but even she came down to the beach with us.

I picked up Sam in the car, now repaired, so he could bring Morgan along. He wasn't sure Morgan would understand, but he'd been fond of Izzy, so it seemed like the right thing to do.

The day was hot and thick and overcast. Every so often there would be the slightest wind, a sigh and nothing more.

I led the group—friends and relatives, a few teachers—to the right spot on the sand. We looked silly in our stiff, formal clothes while fifty feet away on the beach, people lay on Budweiser towels, slathering on coconut oil and praying for sun.

Miguel stood on a slight rise, waiting for a breeze. In his hands he clasped a small blue glass urn. Grasses teased our legs, sand swamped our shoes. Some people sobbed, but no one spoke. We'd already done all the singing and praying and crying we could do.

We waited. The surf churned listlessly. Morgan shifted, Rosa moaned, Gail blew her nose.

Suddenly the grasses began to whisper and move. Two stubby screw pines rocked. A cool wind came to us, blowing our skirts and ties and tangling our hair. Miguel opened the little urn and swooped out his arm and Izzy's ashes caught on the breeze.

We watched, silent and hopeful. I guess we all wanted one of those TV-movie miracles where the clouds open up and the sun pours forth, something nice and symbolic to put a period on the moment. But after a few seconds we realized we were going to have to settle for that half-hearted gust of wind.

Slowly the group dispersed. Sara took Morgan down to the beach to look for shark teeth. Sam came over to me, looking uncomfortable in his suit and tie. "Are you ready to go?" he asked.

"I want to say good-bye to Lauren and Miguel."

"Can you give me a little more time? I was going to see if I could talk to Rosa for a minute."

"Sure."

I watched Sam cross the sand. It was sweet of him to go console Rosa, I thought, and then I remembered that she worked at a nursing home. I wondered if maybe he and his mom had come to some kind of decision about Morgan. We'd barely spoken since that night at the hospital.

Lauren and Miguel and my parents talked for a long time, and then Lauren came over to me. She pulled a manila envelope from her purse. "Izzy wanted me to give you this."

I gave her a hug and then I went to sit at a quiet place near the waves. Inside the envelope was the map of Paris I'd given her. There was a note paper-clipped to the top.

Al—
     You and Sam will be needing this.

Thanks for sharing. I love you,

Iz

I stared at the note for a very long time. She'd known. She might even have known all along. All my worrying about what to tell her, and she'd known.

I laughed out loud. It figured. Iz was way smarter than the rest of us mere mortals.

I searched the beach for Sam. Rosa was writing something on a business card, handing it to him. She patted him on the back, nodding firmly.

"Alison?" My mom was coming, sandals in her hand, bare feet carving holes in the sand. "You okay?"

"Fine," I said, slipping the map into the envelope.

"We're going to go on home, then. Where's Sara?"

"She and Morgan are beachcombing. She can go home with us."

My mom kicked at a shell. "He's a sweet old man, isn't he?"

"Real sweet." I fingered the envelope. "Mom, how would you feel about another pet? Or two?"

She nudged me with her foot. "Please. Like we don't have enough already?"

"I suppose you're right. Of course, Sara could help."

"I believe this is my cue to leave," my mom said.

177

She leaned down and gave me a kiss on the head.

"Just tell me this, then. How do you feel about parrots?"

She took off quickly, hands over her ears. "I can't hear you," she called.

I stood, shading my eyes. Sam was striding across the sand toward Morgan and Sara. Rosa's little white card was in his hand.

"Sara!" I called. "Come here a sec. I've got a proposition for you."

She ran to me and we talked for a while, and then we caught up with Sam and Morgan and made our way across the warm sand. Most of the mourners were already gone. A few stood in the parking lot, talking in low, respectful voices or laughing softly.

I heard someone call my name and turned. Rosa was waving to me from her car. She pulled something from the front seat and joined me on the sand.

"Here," she said, pushing a white sweater into my arms. "I made it for Izzy. I know it's too hot, but next winter, maybe . . ." Her voice fell away.

"It's beautiful, Rosa. Really. Thank you."

She gazed at the beach. Her dark eyes were swollen. Her mouth sagged.

"I hope it was okay," I said. "Coming here, the ashes and everything. It's what Izzy wanted."

"If Izzy wanted to be here—" She fingered her rosary uneasily. "If Izzy wanted it, then it's okay."

I watched her go, then headed to the lot. At the edge of the beach I stopped and turned. I stared at the spot where we had gathered, where Miguel had opened the urn to the wind and Izzy's ashes had taken flight.

I'd been so sure it was important, this ending Izzy had chosen. But now I realized it was just a symbol, a ritual for us, not for her. That wasn't Izzy flying on an updraft, nestled in a clump of sea grass, melting into the waves. We weren't leaving her behind here on the sand.

She was going home with us, where she belonged.

Chapter Fifteen

O N A MIDSUMMER night three months later, the kind where the moon is so bright that sleeping is out of the question, Sam and I went back to Turtle Beach. Many of the loggerhead nests had already hatched, but the one near Izzy's spot was still quiet. We spread out an old blanket I'd brought. I sat between Sam's legs, leaning against his broad chest as if it were a chair, and he put his arms around me and we waited.

I ran my hands along his hard arms and laced my fingers through his. "Maybe tonight," I said. "Most of the others have hatched already."

"Could be a dud," he said, just to provoke me.

"Not here. Not on Izzy's beach."

He parted my hair and trailed kisses down my neck, soft as first rain, and I shivered. I felt like I'd been sitting there all my life. Like nothing on the planet

180

mattered in the least except for the fact that I could feel the steady surge of his heart against my back.

"What did your mom say this morning when she left?" I asked.

"She still wants me to come back to Detroit, but if I want to stay with Jane, it's okay with her. We can work out the school transfer and stuff. Mom told me she understands that I want to stick around and visit Morgan."

"What did you say?"

He brushed his lips against my hair. "I told her that's not the only reason I want to stick around."

"The great beaches, you mean."

He laughed. "Actually, I meant I have to finish up summer school if I intend to be a senior this fall."

I elbowed him and tried to get away and then he was on top of me, kissing me so tenderly I thought I would melt right into the sand and be lost forever. After a while we rolled onto our sides, cupped into each other's warmth, his arms cradling me.

Suddenly Sam jerked up. "What?" I asked.

"The nest."

I sat up on my knees. The spot, carefully marked with stakes to keep out trespassers, was smooth and silent.

"You're hallucinating," I said.

"No, I swear I saw something."

I gave him a dubious look. "You think this is crazy, don't you?"

"Hey, I liked the manatees, remember?"

"You never saw any manatees."

"I saw a milk bottle that bore an amazing resemblance to a manatee."

We lay down again, our eyes on the nest, waiting.

"That time last summer when Iz and I saw them hatch, it was great," I said. "They just pop out of the sand, dozens of these little guys, and go sprinting off to the water. It's amazing."

Sam trailed his fingers down my bare arm. "I miss her," he said.

"Me too," I whispered. "Did you ever come here with Izzy? Like this, at night?"

"No." He stroked my cheek with rough fingertips. "Just you."

"I wish you had," I said. "She would have liked it."

He smiled. "We are one very strange couple, aren't we?"

I turned to him and kissed him, slowly, lingeringly, my hands running over the hard, smooth curves and angles of his body. It wasn't like that first kiss so many months before. This one was big and complicated and full of colors and textures. It held stories in it, and memories, and that made it even better.

Suddenly Sam clutched my arm. "Look. The sand. It's moving."

"Oh, my God, you're right."

"Told you," he said. "Now what?"

"Now we wait some more."

Sam took my hand and kissed my fingers, slowly, tenderly.

"I love you," I said.

"I love you too," he said. "I loved you from that first day you rescued me. And I never stopped."

I smiled. "Have you ever been to Paris, Sam?" I asked, but he didn't have time to answer, because all at once the turtle hatchlings were erupting from the sand as if they were being spewed from a tiny volcano.

They darted toward the water, crazed with life. Their wet, soft shells caught the moonlight and were turned into scampering stars. We watched, laughing, as they made their way across the beach, Izzy's beach, to the dark, vast mystery beyond.

Do you ever wonder about falling in love? About members of the opposite sex? Do you need a little friendly advice but have no one to turn to? Well, that's where we come in . . . Jenny and Jake. Send us those questions you're dying to ask and we'll give you the straight scoop on life and love in the nineties.

DEAR JAKE

Q: *I'm eighteen and really inexperienced. I've only been kissed once, and even that was just a peck! Now I really like this guy at school, and I'm pretty sure he likes me, too. I know for a fact that he's more experienced than I am. Are guys totally repulsed by girls who don't know how to make out? Do you have any advice for me?*

J.P. Rockville, MD

A: My best advice is, Go slowly! Take a while to get to know this guy by just dating casually at first. Don't let the fact that he's gone further than you pressure you into getting more intimate than you want to. Clue him in on how you feel. Chances are he's just as nervous as you are. And most guys aren't bothered by inexperience. In fact, I'm sure this guy will love giving you lessons!

Q: *Lately a guy friend of mine, Jeff, has been hitting on me. I'm a really affectionate person, and we've always hugged, and kissed on the cheek, but now he tries to kiss me on the lips. I'm not interested in Jeff as a boyfriend, but I still love him as a friend.*

How can I get him to leave me alone without ruining our friend-ship? I really need a guy's point of view on this.

C.G. Colorado Springs, CO

A: For starters, it's probably not a great idea to hug and kiss him, no matter how innocent you may think it is. Although there's nothing wrong with being affectionate with friends, at this point he's interpreting your actions the wrong way. Talk to him about other guys, about someone you think is cute or would like to get to know better. Don't flat out tell Stan you're not interested in him, unless he asks. Even then, break it to him gently by saying you don't want to ruin your friendship by getting involved. It's not easy to be dissed; this way you'll be saving his sensitive male ego from a severe bruising!

DEAR JENNY

Q: *My boyfriend and I have been dating for eight months. We had a great relationship until I met Jesse, a guy who lives on my block, about three weeks ago. I'm really attracted to Jesse, but I also love my boyfriend. Help, I'm stuck!*

L.R. Charlotte, NC

A: What a sticky situation! You should get to know Jesse on a friends-only basis, first. If the physical attraction doesn't fade after a few weeks, take it as a sign that something is wrong with your relationship with your boyfriend. Then you need to decide if it's a problem you want to explore and if the two of you can work it out. If not, move on, but I recommend giving yourself some time between boyfriends to recuperate. Breaking up is never an easy thing to do . . . even with another guy waiting in the wings.

Q: *My best friend, Brandi, dates any guy who asks her out. She flirts all the time! Yesterday I went out with Brandi and her boyfriend-of-the-week to a diner, and he and I watched as she flirted with the waiter. She even gave him her phone number! Brandi's habit is really irritating, and she's starting to get a bad reputation. I want to talk to her about it, but whenever I try, she tells me I'm too uptight. Is she right?*

K.A. Shelburne, VT

A: From one woman to another, the answer is no, you're far from being uptight just because you're more selective about whom you date. Brandi's need for attention might be a sign that she's desperate for love and affection. Talk to her without mentioning the fact that her reputation has taken a nosedive. Tell her that she's hurting the guys she dates by flirting in front of them. Ask her if she wants to talk, and tell her that you're willing to listen. Then it's up to her to decide to change or continue to earn the bad reputation she's already achieved.

Do you have questions about love? Write to:
Jenny Burgess or Jake Korman
c/o Daniel Weiss Associates
33 West 17th Street
New York, NY 10011